SAMANTHA ELIZABETH BARRETT

Masquerade
The Battle Within

WestBow
PRESS
A DIVISION OF THOMAS NELSON
& ZONDERVAN

Copyright © 2018 Samantha Elizabeth Barrett.

All rights reserved. No part of this book may be used or reproduced by any means, graphic, electronic, or mechanical, including photocopying, recording, taping or by any information storage retrieval system without the written permission of the author except in the case of brief quotations embodied in critical articles and reviews.

This is a work of fiction. All of the characters, names, incidents, organizations, and dialogue in this novel are either the products of the author's imagination or are used fictitiously.

WestBow Press books may be ordered through booksellers or by contacting:

WestBow Press
A Division of Thomas Nelson & Zondervan
1663 Liberty Drive
Bloomington, IN 47403
www.westbowpress.com
1 (866) 928-1240

Because of the dynamic nature of the Internet, any web addresses or links contained in this book may have changed since publication and may no longer be valid. The views expressed in this work are solely those of the author and do not necessarily reflect the views of the publisher, and the publisher hereby disclaims any responsibility for them.

Any people depicted in stock imagery provided by Thinkstock are models, and such images are being used for illustrative purposes only. Certain stock imagery © Thinkstock.

Scriptures taken from the Holy Bible, New International Version®, NIV®. Copyright © 1973, 1978, 1984, 2011 by Biblica, Inc.™ Used by permission of Zondervan. All rights reserved worldwide.

ISBN: 978-1-9736-0558-4 (sc)
ISBN: 978-1-9736-0559-1 (hc)
ISBN: 978-1-9736-0557-7 (e)

Library of Congress Control Number: 2017916301

Print information available on the last page.

WestBow Press rev. date: 03/05/2018

Note from the Author

Hello there, beautiful readers! I am thrilled that you picked up this book!

When I first told my husband about this book, his question was simple. "What is your purpose?"

Though fiction, Charissa's story is one that many of us will relate to. In fact, Charissa could be you, or your friend, or your co-worker, or your spouse. Her experiences and the experiences of those around her happen every day in our world. My primary purpose in sharing her story is that you would see that, with God's help, you can emerge victorious despite tough circumstances. Her story is far from a fairy tale, as are the stories of those with whom she interacts. Her victory is not a superficial "nothing bad can happen to me because I am a child of God" but rather "I know that though bad things happen, God is with me to help me get back on my feet again" kind of victory.

This book is as much about relying on God to help us fight spiritual battles as it is a message that we do not have to stay where we are. There is no doubt about it – life is hard. Tragedy, both small and large, strikes all walks of life. From teenage break-up, the divorce of our parents, a disagreement with a friend to being a victim of a senseless act of violence, the death of a loved one, a family members' suicide, a battle with cancer, tragedy affects us all. The key to survival is how we respond to the tragedy. We can allow our tragic events to victimize us, and thereby fall prey to their power, becoming powerless to change; or we can recognize that we can choose to become victorious despite our loss, using the loss to build our character and help others through their loss.

My secondary purpose is that, through understanding that we all wear masks to one degree or another, hiding from others the weaknesses we don't want them to see, we can become more empathetic to others who may be fighting battles hidden behind a mask. God created us to be social beings, to befriend and mentor, and to encourage one another through tough times. Although we may, from time to time, feel we are failing at our mission, to understand one another, and be a rock to someone else when they need it while having a rock when we need one is a key factor of success in life. We are here to help one other thrive.

Lastly, my purpose through this project is to connect with people. If you are impacted by this book in any way, I would love to hear from you! Please check out my blog at www.journey-for-life.com, or email me at sbjourneyforlife@gmail.com.

Blessings to you!
SB

PS. If you have suicidal thoughts, please, please, please, reach out to someone for help. Call the National Suicide Prevention Hotline at 1-800-273-8255. Find a pastor, therapist, or friend with whom to share your feelings in order to get help.

CHAPTER 1

The Battle Begins Again

The spiritual battle rages inside my head, consuming my thoughts like a fire consuming a bush. The fiery inferno burns hot and wild and for all practical purposes, it appears as though Satan is winning. The battle started in a dream a couple of days before my 40th birthday... The details of the dream escape me now, except for the last moments before I awoke. Feeling desperate, nurses around me quickly wheeled the gurney down the hall of the hospital. Looking up, all I could see were bright lights and nurses wearing facemasks, hurrying down the hallway hollering, "We need more serotonin! We need more serotonin! The serotonin level is dropping!" Their concern was as if the patient's serotonin level was a matter of life or death. I could sense their feeling of hopelessness as the serotonin level continued to drop. Then I woke up.

Strange dream, I thought. I had been having strange dreams for about a year now – so much so that I started a dream book in the spring – recording all of the dreams that I had as soon after I woke up as possible because sometimes when too much time passed, I could no longer remember them. The dreams I had that spring were extremely vivid. Often my dreams were about people being murdered, though rarely were they people that I actually know. There were several dreams where the murderer was the same individual – I can clearly see his face, but I do not know him. Tall and thin, with black hair turning gray around his ears, his full gray mustache gives him a distinguished yet menacing appearance.

The murder dreams lasted for several months… and then I entered a period where I could no longer remember my dreams. My dream journal turned stale, and I became frustrated. I love dreams – always have, especially the strange ones. They always seemed to me the minds way of escaping the world around them.

On the morning that I woke up to the strange serotonin dream, I suddenly felt like there was a dark cloud above me. I found my zeal for life diminishing, eventually disappearing. Me, of all people…. Energetic and passionate, eager to be the change that I wanted to see in people. I found myself on the edge of despair wondering if life was even worth the effort. Later that morning, I found myself crying in the middle of the church service for no apparent reason. Yes, I know that there was a problem with the sound equipment the day before. One of the students damaged a speaker as we hauled it from the park back to the church. I felt bad about it, but not to the point of tears. I really could not explain why my emotions were so suddenly spiraling out of control like a runaway train just before it jumps the tracks. I had learned to control my emotions many years ago when I made a conscious choice to ignore them. In those quiet moments of the church service, my emotions betrayed me, just as Judas had betrayed Jesus.

I replayed the previous day over in my head. It was an awesome day –we had just finished a week of vacation bible school – I taught the pre-school age kids music – they loved it! About fifteen children had accepted Christ as their Savior for the first time in their young lives. The weather was beautiful. The kids in the youth band were excited to play. I had talked with all of the sound technicians and had someone lined up to run sound at the park. Somehow, in that communication, I either assumed or forgot to mention explicitly to Pastor Charles or PJ that the soundman recommended the equipment from Children's Church. I thought that I had all bases covered. However, when we were loading the equipment, Pastor Charles came over to ask if we were going somewhere. Thinking he knew about the VBS picnic (and since it was PJ's wife who asked me if the youth band could play), I was sort of surprised, but remembered how much he does not like surprises, so I muttered something about being sorry I did not talk with him first, but that the sound guys were prepared for the day. One of the kids helping to load equipment was having trouble getting one of the stands to collapse. Pastor Charles helped him lift the speaker off the stand so that it could fit in the van. Finally, we were able to get everything loaded, and headed over to the park.

We had a great time playing that day and received many compliments from people at the picnic. I was very proud of those kids. After dinner, we broke down the equipment to load it up once more and return it to church. As we were loading, someone was again having trouble collapsing the stand for the speakers. One of the kids was trying to wrestle it off. When I noticed him, I immediately asked him to stop. I thought that we could simply load it in the van as it was and it could fit from front to back without being collapsed, but one of the other kids was able to collapse the unit. When we got back to the church and were setting up all of the equipment, someone noticed that the bottom of one of the speakers was "caved in". Immediately, I called my soundman and explained what had happened. Joshua called PJ, who was somewhat irritated with him. In hindsight, I should have asked Joshua not to call his dad and talked with PJ myself. However, I think he was afraid to get in trouble himself. At any rate, when I talked to Adam, he said, "oh, yeah, I know that those speakers have the wrong size cup for the poles that are with the stands. I probably just need to get a new cup for them". Ok – cool. Not as bad as I thought? I went home, exhausted from the week, looking for a good night sleep. That was "serotonin" dream night.

I have been working with the youth band for the past

year – a few months after Lisa asked me to. Lisa was one of the other musicians at the church who were working with the youth band for several years. She told me last year that she felt she had "aged out" (whatever that means) and could not really relate to them anymore, but that she felt they could relate to me. "No way", I told her when she originally approached me at Creation 2009 with that idea. That is all I need is for Lisa to feel like I took her job away. I dismissed her request at the time, until a few months later, when she came back and asked me again, saying that she really did not want to do it anymore – that she just couldn't take working with the kids anymore. I thought and prayed about it – and talked with Pastor Ian about it, who seemed to think it might be a great idea. Last September I started working with them. I really wanted to make a difference in their lives – to give them something worth playing for – to put their talents to work. I had visions of what the youth band could do – we would be awesome and have awesome rehearsals and worship. Sometimes working with the kids was frustrating – they were unreliable, and irregular in their practice attendance, but then they would say or do something that would tell me that all of the time spent was worth it. In addition, it would remind me that I really just want to make a difference in their lives – to have them someday come back to me and say that they are where they are spiritually in part because of the work that I was doing.

I love Jesus – and he had carried me through the times in my life that I was so despondent to want to take my own life. That's why I believed in groups like "to write love on her arms" and in Let Go Let God – because I KNOW that He healed me from my depression years ago – and from the anger that I felt over losing my dad; and I know that he can help these kids, too. This is the reason I eagerly agreed to volunteer for LGLG. I know God can make a difference in the lives of these kids. There were amazing changes in the lives of these kids – especially Aubrey. The past year has been a struggle. Nevertheless, I see the difference that God is making – and so excited that He is using me to do it – these kids are learning to trust me. At the end of it all, that was what was important – to show Christ to these kids.

When Pastor Charles called me into his office, wondering why the tears, I really could not answer him. I really did not know. I could have made up some story about something going on at home – knowing what I have talked to him about years prior; it really would not have surprised him. However, I did not – I just really did not know what to say, so I said that it must have been about the speakers. I knew it really was not, but it seemed like the most logical thing to say at the time. He told me briefly about all of the things that had happened within the past week – the door being ripped off the wall in the men's bathroom, the gas-line that was struck during the digging for the new sign, and explained that sometimes these things are just a test. He knew that I had called Adam already about fixing it. He said he felt I acted responsibly and just need to understand that sometimes these things happen. I know it should have made me feel better, but it did not. I still could not explain what was wrong. Since that time, I have had this sort of ominous, ethereal feeling about me that I cannot really explain, but unmistakably tells me that I am not making a difference for God – that I should stop trying.

I took a vacation day from work on my birthday and took the kids to Water World. I love it there, almost as much as the beach. Celebrating my birthday there with the kids was perfect. I stood in line for the water slides; on the verge of tears all day long, thankful for my dark sunglasses that hid my tear-filled eyes… was it the fact that I was turning 40? I never really cared about age before. Forty sounds old, truly old, but I really do not care… I decided long ago that young is a state of mind, and I would always be young in mind. Turning forty did not make me sad. Was it the "serotonin" dream? I wondered.

I sent a text to my friend, Jim, a police officer. I asked him whether police officers investigate suicide scenes. He told me they investigate every kind of death. I asked him on average how many suicides there are in Pleasantville each year... he said about 10-12. A little while later, Jim texted me to tell me he responded to a call about a suicide that afternoon. "Interesting coincidence", we agreed. I wondered if he wondered why I had asked the question. He never asked.

Usually able to ignore her rude comments and obnoxious digs in the past, I have grown increasingly irritated with Lisa. In fact, I remember when Martin Cottman came to visit about a year or so after he moved away. He told me I have made him proud because I have stepped into his shoes quite nicely at LIFE Church. Furthermore, he recognized that I am quite capable of "handling Lisa". Those were his exact words. I kind of laughed about it at the time and dismissed it as no big deal, but everyone knows that Lisa can be difficult sometimes. Even Lisa knows that about herself. However, when she talks about the fact that she knows she is difficult to work with, she does it with an attitude that screams, "If you do not like it, too bad. I have no intention of trying to change it – if you do not like it; it is your problem, not mine". I have been unable to shake her attitude lately. Since the "serotonin" day when she threw me under the bus in front of Pastor Charles. We met with Pastor Charles in between the first and second service, (after Pastor Charles had asked me about the tears) she and Adam and I, to talk with Pastor Charles about some of the logistics of moving to 3 Sunday services. During the meeting, she pointed an accusatory finger at me and said, "Well *she* won't step down!" I do not remember much of the rest of the meeting. I was in complete dismay. You want me to step down? Step down? I have been playing the piano in church since I was seventeen years old. This is a talent that God gave me, and the only way that I really know how to honor Him. No, I had not really ever thought about stepping down, mostly because I enjoy playing music. I always felt as if there was always room for many musicians - I mean, the more the merrier, right? Nevertheless, I will show you that I will step down if that is what you want me to do. ..... Maybe I should step down. Maybe that is what everyone wants me to do, and I have just been too stupid to realize it..... Yeah, that is probably it. I've probably been so wrapped up in my own desire to please God and make up for all the years that I was not honoring Him that I've allowed my desire to play music for Him to unknowingly create a problem? Hmm..... I would have to think more about that.

    I dwelled on that comment for a few days. It ate at me, and I could feel the bitterness welling up inside me. I resented it. Wednesday was youth group night. I did not want to go but went anyway out of a sense of obligation. It was Parker's last evening with us, and he was leading music – he wanted me to play with him. As our summer intern, Parker expressed enthusiasm about the ministry into which he was entering. He had experienced all facets of church ministry this summer and was finishing his assignment by leading worship for youth group. He had selected a few songs that I knew only from the local Christian radio station. His wonderful smile and eagerness to teach new songs to the youth were an inspiration to me. Despite spiritual battle raging inside me, the worship was awesome on this evening.

    After youth group ended, I gathered my things, including the lyric sheets of the new music that Parker had shared, and headed out into the dusk. Headed straight for me as I walked out the door was Lisa. I tried to avoid her but was unable to. "Hello," she said. I shallowly returned the hello, not interested in conversation. I continued the short walk to my car. Then she did something that completely surprised me. She told me that she was sorry for throwing me under the bus. We had a short conversation about it – I told her that I was really struggling with it. She told me that she knows that she is a brat; she has always been that way, and when she gets angry about something, she will lash out to hurt someone – she said she has done it to Pastor Charles to the point where he pounded his fist on a table one time. She told me that she was angry that I came to church on Sunday early when she was on the schedule to be there. I barely remembered the incident. Because I am so used to always being there to play – I have done it for twenty-three years now. My kids were singing the VBS songs in church today anyway, so I brought them to the early service. When I saw her at church that Sunday, she asked me what I wanted to do… so I just said, "Awe, why don't you just go ahead and sit through the service". I did not even think anything of it – I actually thought that I was doing her a favor. She previously asked me to remove her from the schedule as much as possible during the summer. I took her request at face value and granted her wish. However, I discovered she did not really want to be removed from the schedule. She really just wanted me to go after her and say, "But Lisa, we really need you ON the schedule". I thought I was doing what she wanted – or at least what she said she wanted.

I do not like games. I do not like to play them. I have always been very open and honest with my thoughts and my feelings, and am most comfortable in the presence of others who do the same. I do not try to read into what people might actually be meaning when they say something to me – I take it for face value. If you tell me that you want to participate in music, use you I will. If you tell me you do not want to participate, I will not use you. Simple. Lisa did not really want it that way. Because of this, she was angry when we went into the meeting with Pastor Charles. Instead of simply saying, "no, really, I'm here, I'd like to go ahead and play", she stewed about it until our meeting. Then WHAM-O – she hit me on the head.

Therefore, there I was… standing in the parking lot having Lisa apologize to me. I know Christ forgave me for all I have done and because of that, I am obligated to forgive others. I know this, but I am really struggling with this. Frankly, I just want to stay out of Lisa's way. Her vindictiveness is exhausting to me. I have been hurt so much by those I love in the past eighteen months; I am not interested in being hurt more. Therefore, I told her that I had no choice but to forgive her. In addition, I told her that I serve my Jesus and not her…to which she replied, "thank God". We hugged and went our separate ways. Inside I am still struggling with it. I have been praying and asking God to help me let it go – because I want to honor Him..... However, He feels so far away. Where did He go? Where did I go? Usually, when this sort of thing happens, there is something that happens, or a drifting apart. Just a week ago, I felt absolutely on fire to do His will. What happened?

It was an interesting conversation with Pastor Charles on Saturday at Olivia's birthday party. He noticed my hoodie said, "To Write Love on Her Arms" and questioned me what that meant. "It is an anti-suicide organization", I replied. "Interesting", he said. "Did you know that suicides are on the rise with women? It used to be that women would attempt suicide, but fail - because they did not really want to die, they really just wanted someone to help them.... Moreover, when a man attempted suicide, he had already made his mind up to succeed... and he usually did. However, research shows that is going the other way now... more women are succeeding. There was a case that I was called out to recently – young, successful women – did not want to create a mess for her family – took the time to lay plastic out on the floor surrounding her. She smoked a cigarette and ate a piece of candy (as evidenced by the wrapper on the table), and proceeded to shoot herself. The problem was that she fell the opposite way from the plastic. The best-laid plans of mice and men..."

Wow. How thoughtful of her. When I had previously considered the means by which I might take my life, and thought briefly about a gun or cutting... I always dismissed it as creating too much of a mess for those left behind. It never occurred to me to lay plastic out.

"I had two neighbors commit suicide", I said.

"Is that right? Both of them women?" Pastor Charles said in disbelief.

"Yes, one when I was just a kid – the woman up the street shot herself.... And then there was Morgan, our next door neighbor, who OD'd." I thought back to the day that Morgan took her life. Morgan had always had issues – mostly, it seemed, with self-esteem. She was afraid to drive her car at night and afraid to drive in the snow. Nice person. My sister and I babysat her kids. They moved in when the oldest child was two – I was probably thirteen or fourteen. Morgan's husband, Brice, left them during what seemed to be his mid-life crisis. Morgan was devastated at first, but as the months wore on, she appeared to be getting stronger and stronger. She had lost a lot of weight and looked terrific. I remember seeing her at a graduation party a few months before her death. I told her she looked terrific... She made some kind of comment about his leaving, and I made some kind of comment about it being good for her. You remember these things after someone has taken their own life.... You grieve, and you think about the fact that you could have and should have seen it coming and done something to stop it, but you did not.

I was thinking that if I planned my suicide again, I would keep it completely a secret and make sure that I succeeded. I really would not want anyone to save me. I have read that those who are planning their suicide and are sure about it are completely at peace – and they seem so much better to everyone around them, just before they take that final step. That is the masquerade. That is why sometimes people who have always been a wreck suddenly seem strong – like Morgan did.

"There was the couple from my old church who made a suicide pact with each other to drink themselves to death", I continued. "She succeeded but he did not. However, a few weeks after her funeral, he succeeded in taking his own life. It was very sad". Yes, I have known many people who had committed suicide, I thought. There was Mr. McCutcheon, whose son found him, and Beth, and Peggy, and Morgan, and Rob and Missy, and someone I worked with… and the list goes on. I have known many. In fact, I wrote a song about it a long time ago – and played it at one of the piano concerts that I gave at Emerson Methodist church. Its title is "Follow Me Now"

Follow Me Now

Cold, rainy nights,
With only fear to hold me tight
Only a teardrop to keep me company
As I lay there crying, it seemed nobody cared,
But I did not hear You calling out to me.

Tears pouring out,
Each one of them a cry of pain
Reaching out for someone to share the pain
As I yelled into the silence, it seemed nobody cared,
But I did not hear you calling out to me.

Won't you please take my hand, and follow me?
I will take you where you can be free
I will wipe all the tears away from your face
If you'll only come and follow Me now

Reaching for you
Wanting you to hold me tight
Comforting me when nothing else seems right
As I give you my pain to let you comfort me
I did not' hear your voice calling out to me.

Won't you please take my hand, and follow me?
I will take you where you can be free
I will wipe all the tears away from your face
If you'll only come and follow me now?

See, I know the Truth. I know that Jesus hears our every cry, and feels our every pain, and loves us, and sees us through the hard times... and delivers us from evil, etc. etc. I KNOW that with my head.... However, I cannot feel it in my heart. Why does He feel so far away? I know that it is because I have moved, not because He has... but why can I not seem to get back to Him? I know this with my head.... I have to hold on to what I know is true, even if my emotions are telling me a lie, until I can get my feet back under me again.... I am not sure what knocked them out from underneath me, but I need to find a way to get them back underneath me. I need to rely on Jesus to see me through again.... It is what I have told Aubrey for months now. I just need to do it myself. Why is it so hard? When will it subside? Moreover, it if it so hard for me, who has known the Truth for so many years, how hard must it be for those who are not even sure of the Truth yet. My heart bleeds for them.

CHAPTER 2

The Silence of God

"Given the news, I started this morning's staff meeting with; I thought I would share this quote I read today. Days like today are days that this really rings true. Spend it wisely!"

> *' Life is a coin. You can spend it any way you wish, but you can only spend it once.'*

This email came from my boss at 5 pm today. He started his staff meeting today with the news that two people associated with our company passed away over the weekend. The first was a former purchasing agent. I knew him in name from a previous company that I worked with, but not directly. The second was Carson's wife Cathy. I knew she had been battling lymphoma for several years now – same cancer that killed my dad in 1979. I had seen Carson about a month ago and asked how she was doing. He just gave a quick shake of his head from side to side and did not say much. Carson was always fun – I liked him from the time that I started working at Conradia. He had aged so much in the past few years that the vibrant, reckless engineer was almost unrecognizable. I could hardly hold back the tears in the staff meeting today. I will go to the viewing to offer my support to Carson and his fifteen-year-old son. I grieve as I think what he is going through right now; I have been there myself. It brings back a flood of memories of the day my dad died from lymphoma. All these years later, it feels like it was yesterday.

I went home for a quick bite and then a school meeting with my son. Since David is entering middle school this year, the program is a little different – the meeting was to explain how it all works. After the meeting, David asked if we could go out for dessert. I had been planning to take him home and then go over to the funeral home to pay my respects to Carson, but when I looked at my son, I decided it was more important to spend the time with him. David is the child who is most like me. I worry about him sometimes. When he was 5 years old, one time, he was so distraught by something that happened that he went and pulled a steak knife out of a drawer, put it on his wrists and shouted, "Well, maybe I'll just kill myself!" "NO!" I remember thinking at the time. PLEASE do not have the same struggles as me. I could not even imagine how a five-year-old could have that idea – it was nothing we had ever talked about in our home. How would a five-year-old know that people kill themselves by cutting their wrists? So many times over the years since that day, David and I have talked about wanting and needing to find someone to talk to about the things that bother him – and perhaps we needed to find a good counselor. He never wanted to do that because he was so afraid that people would think he was nuts…. I guess deep down I, too, was afraid that people would think we were nuts. I have asked him if he would like to come to Let Go Let God, and I think he considered somewhat but has not yet decided to go. So we went to Eat n' Park and had dessert. As we ate our luscious chocolate cake dessert, I wondered how deep the impact of my death would be on him. I thought about Clay, Carson's fifteen-year-old son, now dealing with the loss of his mother. I remember that feeling. It stinks. I do not want my son to have to experience that feeling. Hmmm… is there ever really a good time to die? I wondered.

Masquerade

I had thought about suicide from time to time during my life. My earliest recollection was when I was around twelve or thirteen years old, and I just did not see a purpose for my life. I recently found the journal that I kept during those years, and was astonished as I read page after page, entry after entry, of how I knew in my head that God was there, but he felt so far away from me that I could not find him. I wrote about the things that I regretted doing, the sins I regrettably committed. I survived those tumultuous teenage years and eventually finished college and got married. Two and a half years after our wedding, we had our first baby, followed by another just eleven months after. During their toddler years, the thoughts of suicide returned. I had even planned my death several times, but stopped only because I knew, in my heart, my suicide would have a devastating effect on my children. There was no other reason that kept me from it. On some days, I thought about what my husband's reaction would be – would he see that he contributed to my feeling hopeless? Would my friends and family feel they should have done something differently to prevent it – just how I felt when Morgan died? It was ironic to me that all of the feelings I felt as a teenager had resurfaced years later in my life. I thought that when I asked Jesus to come and live in my heart that the old things were gone, never to resurface again. I was wrong. There were times in my life that were hard, and it seemed like Satan was using those things to remind me about the desperation that I felt before Christ was Lord of my life. It was as if Satan was trying to tell me that Jesus really did not save me. The demonic force was so powerful that I think there were times when I doubted it myself. These thoughts flooded my head as David and I enjoyed our desserts.

Later that night, after the kids went to bed, I went on the computer to check my emails. I could hardly believe the one I saw from Cooper M. It is Suicide Prevention week – who knew? He sent an email to alert people to seek help if they felt they needed it. Cooper helps with Let Go Let God. I met him last year when the program began. A retired marine, he struggled with alcohol until he got help and met his Savior – now he is interested in helping the kids at LGLG too. How awesome is that?

So I logged into Facebook to catch up on everyone's status updates. Some of the things people post are ridiculous, but I love to see what is going on in everyone's life. Even those who I have not seen since high school, it is good to catch up with periodically. I like that they are on FB. I can talk with them if I choose, or not if I choose, and I can keep a casual eye on what is going on in their life. While I am on there, I see that Pastor Dwayne had just posted a video. He is not on FB very often – and I remembered I wanted to ask him about something – actually, so many times in the past couple of weeks I wanted to reach out to him to ask him to pray for me… and then chickened out because I do not really want to talk about how I feel. I messaged him to say hi. He says Hi and then says to check out this song from Andrew Peterson. I do not know Andrew Peterson, but when I heard this song, I wondered how he could possibly know me; know what I am feeling right now; and how he could have written these words that shook my soul to the core. The songs' title is "The Silence of God". How could Dwayne have known that I needed to hear those words at exactly this moment? I had not spoken to Dwayne in months, and yet, he messaged me and pointed me to words that I desperately needed to hear. These words, Andrew Parker's words, so raw, so true, exemplified the thoughts running through my mind – the thoughts that I could not articulate, but were consuming me like fire.

> It is enough to drive a man crazy; it'll break a man's faith
> It is enough to make him wonder if he's ever been sane
> When he's bleating for comfort from Thy staff and Thy rod
> And the heaven's only answer is the silence of God

The silence of God…. That is what I hear now. The silence is deafening. I can see that God is trying to show me that he cares through signs, as the one Pastor Dwayne gave me tonight. I have been crying out to Him to help me for weeks now and just cannot seem to get my footing. I cannot hear him! I wondered if Morgan had ever cried out to God and only heard the lonesome echo.

You see, I know in my head that God sees the struggle that I'm going through – and He's sending me one sign after another to show me that He cares for me… and that there might even be people who care for me, but my emotions betray me – and tell me I'm unlovable, unable to make an impact.

I decided to reach out to Dwayne by asking him a question about spiritual warfare – is it possible that I am being attacked? He responded very quickly – "Absolutely – and because the devil knows he cannot win the big war, he tries his hardest to win all of the battles he can – and doesn't fight fair." Then in all capital letters, Dwayne wrote, "but SATAN CANNOT WIN!"

The silence of God… Where is He, anyway? I have been trying to call him, and He is not answering me… it is agonizing.

I asked Dwayne to pray for me, and he said he would. As I was chatting with him, a message popped up on my screen from my friend, Brianna. Brianna is sixteen years old. I have been praying for Brianna for about eight years now since I first started attending LIFE church. I learned of her during a Wednesday night Bible study, when I met her grandmother, who had asked for prayer for her. Brianna's parents were going through a divorce at the time. I liked the name Brianna, so the prayer request was easy to remember more than any prayer request, I think. Therefore, over the years, I would think of her and keep praying for her. Occasionally, I would see her at church, and I would smile at her and tell her I was praying for her.

She came to the junior high retreat last year – my first year as a youth sponsor, and Nicole's first year in youth group. We had gotten to know each other – I had told her several times that I have been praying for her for a long time. I think she thought I was crazy. Brianna and I became FB friends earlier this year. Usually, late at night, she would message me to say hi. Last weekend, we were chatting and she mentioned that she had gotten a necklace engraved with Trenton, 1979-1994.

"Who's Trenton?" I asked. "My brother", she replied. "What happened to him?" I asked, not sure what to expect. "Suicide", she replied. Wow. That is almost unbelievable considering I have heavily contemplated it in the week just past. In my head, I know that sometimes people who are close to someone who has committed suicide, they may be more likely to try it themselves; and I know that Brianna has been struggling for the past year with her "religion", and her family (who wants nothing to do with her "religion"). She recently shared with me that her father is an alcoholic who is abusive when he drinks, and she is worried about him because the doctor told him that he is going to die if he does not change, but he does not want to change. I am very worried that Brianna might look at the choices Trenton made and decide to do the same.

I have two IM's going at once…. In one, I am reaching out to my friend for help; in the other, my friend is reaching out to me for help. Ironic, is it not? So "bipolar". With Brianna, I instantly go into "respond with what I know in my head" mode…. Do not let her see that you are on the verge of suicide. So…. I copy and paste what my friend Dwayne just sent me – that SATAN CANNOT WIN. I copy and paste because they are not my words – I was not even sure I believed them at that moment in time, but somehow I knew I had to be a rock for Bri, just as Dwayne was being a rock for me. Brianna and I go on to have an online conversation about the fact that God is there for her – and Jesus will never fail her even when it seems everyone around her does. I ask her to come to LGLG. She already talked with John about that – and planning to come. Great. Hopefully, we can both get help there, I thought. For that moment, I keep up the masquerade, not because I want Brianna to think I am something I am not, but because she is depending on me now, and I cannot let her down.

CHAPTER 3

The Roger Factor

Who is your Roger? Are there any Roger's in your life? It is an interesting question. The movie, "To Save a Life" came out in the spring of 2009. Our church went to see it at a local movie theater. Pastor Ian worked with several other youth groups in the area to persuade the movie theater to bring the movie there. They reluctantly agreed, but only if the youth pastors would commit to selling 1000 seats – and just for 1 weekend. All of the youth pastors worked together to get as many people as possible to see the movie – and every showing was packed. They ended up showing it for two weekends!

The movie starts with a scene from the funeral of a high school student who had taken his life by shooting himself in the head in the school hallway. At the funeral is one of the high school's basketball stars – a kid who we later learned was a friend of the deceased when they were young. Through a series of choices, and the desire to be popular, Jake had abandoned the friendship he once shared with Roger, who now lay in the casket. Jake wondered if he could have made a difference in Roger's life.

The movie was so moving. We could actually feel what Jake was feeling. For me, it brought back all of the memories of how I felt when Morgan died – I should have known, but I did not – probably because I was too thoughtless. For a while, it inspired the kids in our youth group to be on the lookout for "Roger's" in their life.

In May, we showed the movie again at our church. I brought the kids again. I cannot sit through the movie without crying. I hate crying. I hate emotions.

I am so proud of Keith. He IS Jake. He is a basketball star who was searching for meaning in his life since his father passed away from cancer several years ago. I met Keith when he joined the youth band to sing. Great kid. He gave his testimony that night in May, after the movie. He was that person who was searching for meaning – looking for it in alcohol and girls, just like Jake. Because of one faithful friend who prayed for him and waited quietly for the right opportunity to invite him to church, his life was forever changed. One night, after drinking with his friends, Keith came home. His mom asked him pointedly, "What are you doing with your life?" He could not answer. She asked him if he would like to go back to church. He thought about the little church they attended in Clover Ridge. No, he really did not want to go back there – I mean, the services were fine, but they just did not do anything for me. "Well, what about the church in Pleasantville where they do the Biker Blessing?" They showed up the next day.

Still hungover from the night before, Keith slumped into the pew right in front of Tim. During the greeting time, Tim shook Keith's hand – he was so excited to see him there. Keith later described how he felt when he realized how excited Tim was to see him. Inside of Tim, he was jumping for joy that God had answered his prayer and brought Keith to church. Keith began to come to youth group and eventually gave his life to Christ. Now, here he was giving his testimony to 120 people. Because of the love that Tim showed, and the love that he found in Christ, Keith was able to reach out to Luke, a kid who seemed to have no friends…. Now Luke was coming to youth group, and Christ was making a difference in his life.

Magical. People who say that they cannot see God working are just not able to see the things like this that make Him so real. He DOES care about each one of us. He does. I know this in my head... and I have seen it. Why can I not feel it?

Keith is at college now. Colorado. He graduated from high school in June. I was worried that the college environment would be hard on his faith, but his posts on Facebook are an indication that his faith is stronger than ever. I am so proud of him. Last weekend, he came home on break and gave the message during the youth service. It was amazing. He is really going to make a difference for God. Someday, he will make a nice, young woman very happy.

I wondered if anyone would recognize that I am a Roger. Do I want anyone to see that? Not really. It is part of the masquerade. The masquerade is necessary sometimes, to carry us through the thirsty times until we can drink the Living Water again. Why are the eyes so willing to tell what the lips would not dare?

CHAPTER 4

Window Pains

The impact of Morgan's death on the kids must have been devastating. Funny, they were exactly the same ages as my sister and me when my dad died, eight and ten. I tried to keep involved in their lives as they got older, especially Lindsay's. I taught her piano lessons. I invited her over to our house to carve pumpkins, make cookies, and dye Easter Eggs. Her father, Brice, never once asked me where we lived. I would always pick her up and take her back home again. It irritated me that he never asked. Our kids were not big enough yet to go to someone's house without us, but I could not imagine letting my nine or ten-year-old go to someone's house without knowing where they lived. One night, I was taking her home to an empty house, she told me that she is often in the house alone and afraid. My mom still lived next door to Lindsay. I told her that anytime she wanted, she could go next door to hang out with my mom. I knew my mom would not mind that. My heart ached for Lindsay, and I prayed for her regularly that someone, at some point in her life, would introduce her to Jesus.

Morgan used to play the piano. Something else that I regret: She quit playing the piano because of me. We never had air conditioning in the house I grew up in, so during the summer, the windows and sliding glass door were always open with screens on them. I remember one time when I was a teenager that Morgan told me she used to play the piano – she did not play anymore because she could hear me play through the open windows of our house, and she did not want me to hear how badly she played in comparison. I was devastated. That cursed gift.

I have never thought of playing music as a competition – God gives music to many people – and to those who enjoy music, I would not ever want to deprive them of that. I always felt so bad about the fact that some people looked at it differently. After her death, I began to teach Lindsay how to play the piano. She wanted to learn to play like her mother. I was delighted, and taught Lindsay lessons for a while, until one day out of the clear blue, Brice sold the piano.

How could he *do* that to Lindsay? I wanted her to be able to play like her mother – and she wanted to play like her mother – and he took that away from her, just like that. No warning. No explanation. Just took it away from her. She was devastated.

Shortly after that happened, Brice picked up the family and moved to Florida. I tried to keep in touch with Lindsay – even sent her pre-paid phone cards to be able to call me…. However, she never did. Finally, after years of trying, I gave up keeping in touch with her; but she never left my heart. I continued to think about her from time to time, wondering how her life turned out – what did she do for a living. Did her brother turn out okay? Did Brice ever get married again? Did she ever find Jesus?

The overwhelming feeling that I have had recently is that I should give music up completely. The feeling seems to be strongest on Sunday evenings when I sink deeper into this gripping depression than before. There must be a reason this is happening on Sunday… As I reflect back on the impact that my music had on Morgan – to cause her to give up something she once loved, I cannot help but feel this is an affirmation that I should give up that which has become my escape from reality.

Funny, I have played music for my entire life – since before I started taking piano lessons at age 4. For a long, long time, I took for granted the gift of music. I played in several bands from the time I was 12 until about 17, sometimes played in bars with those bands. My mother was disappointed in this. I recall times when she would warn me that if I did not honor God with the gift He gave me, He would take it away. She warned that perhaps something bad would happen to my hands and I would be unable to play. From time to time, I reflected on this. At the time, I thought it was horrific for a parent to hold this "God threat" over my head. I mean, would God really do that? Now as I looked back on it, I am thankful that I have grown spiritually to know that sometimes God does allow seemingly bad things to happen to people, but, just like Romans 8:28 says, He uses those things to bring about changes He wants to see in us because He loves us so much.

I thought back to when I played in the orchestra for, "You're a Good Man, Charlie Brown". It was the summer of 1987. I had a great time rehearsing for that performance and was excited about the fact that my boyfriend, Andrew, was going to come and see it. During one scene, Schroeder plays and sings a song to the tune of the Moonlight Sonata, the first movement. I was to continue on to play the 2nd and 3rd movements as piano solos. This would be the first time Andrew would hear me really play a piano solo. I was excited and nervous about that. As the show began, I looked around nervously to see if I could see him, but he had not yet arrived. About halfway through my solo, Andrew showed up with one of his friends. I was devastated that he could not show up on time. I fought back tears as I played Beethoven's rich composition, doing my best to perform well under the circumstances. After the show, there were people who told me it was fabulous, but I knew it was not my best. I was devastated that he had broken my heart. Little did I know then, it was the first of many heartbreaks.

When I was fifteen years old, I studied music with Johann Rummo, Professor Emeritus at Boston University School of Music, who had a profound effect on my musical development. He enabled me to unleash my passion for music, and pour all of myself into everything that I played. I had to audition just for the privilege Years after I had stopped taking piano lessons from him, returning to Boston U. for a visit, Johann shared with me that his only granddaughter had committed suicide. She was only seventeen, and the impact of her death was devastating on her mother, and on Johann and his wife.

When I was seventeen, I became a church accompanist and choir director at Emerson Methodist Church, a role I would play all through college... Music was in my veins... Yet, perhaps that is exactly what I need to do: Just give it up. Do not listen to it or play it. Maybe I am hurting people with this gift.

Remembering some of those memories was a little bit painful for me, but as I sat in despair, contemplating giving up music forever, I could hardly fathom what my life would be like without music. For the first time in my life, every single note that I played was to the Glory of God. What could I give back to God if it was not music?

The week after Lisa threw me under the bus was the Steve Jones concert. Steve Jones was a musician who had played under the stage name of Joey Catman with some of the history's most well-known entertainers. At the 500 Club in Atlantic City back in the 60's and 70's, Joey sang with the likes of Ray Charles, Sammy Davis Junior, and Jerry Lee Lewis. The son of a pastor, Steve hit rock bottom one night after his wife and young daughter had left him. On a train headed to nowhere, thinking about taking his own life, he caught the sight of an old country church, and something inside him grabbed a hold. He gave his life to Christ and has been singing for Him ever since. He was coming to our church. Pastor Charles asked me to play some music before the show began – and even possibly accompany him on a song or two while he was here. Just days after Lisa asked me to forgive her; I was meeting with Steve to go over the songs he wanted to sing. The evening was beautiful. Joe came to play the drums and Kevin on the trumpet.

Kevin is amazing. Joe was terrific. We played with Steve as he sang a few of the old hymns. The audience really seemed to like it. Steve seemed to enjoy it, too. I received many compliments about the evening. Afterward, I wondered if this was God's way of showing me, I should continue music. The following Sunday, even Lisa complimented me, again apologizing and telling me that she knew I was in my element when I was playing for Steve on Friday evening. Was this God trying to tell me something? I could not tell. I cannot hear him. He is too far away from me.... Alternatively, am I too far away from him?

CHAPTER 5

Blade

It is interesting how things come about in life. Several months ago, I received a friend request on Facebook from Allison Rae. I did not know her but saw that we had a mutual friend. I quickly learned through her status updates and wall that she struggles with cutting and self-mutilation. Another candidate for LGLG, I thought. She and I have had a couple of conversations back and forth (all initiated by her) about whether or not God exists and/or cares about her. Awesome opportunity. I told her I would love for her to come to youth group – or if she wanted to meet for coffee sometime, I would share with her the Jesus that I have come to know and love.

Last Friday, my daughter, Nicole went to the high school football game. When she came home, she was pretty excited telling me about all of the people that she saw there – lots of people from our church, etc.... it reminded me of the days that Eileen and I used to go to the Happy Valley football games – had a great time walking around and socializing by the concession stand... I do not remember watching much of the games... Andrew does not feel that Nikki should be going to football games in 7th grade. I do not see what the big deal is. At any rate, during this discussion with Nikki, she told me about the police arresting a girl named Allison.

"Allison Rae?" I asked. She said, "You *know* her?" I pulled up her profile picture on Facebook, and she said, "Yeah, that's her! I cannot believe you are her friend. Everyone is afraid of her. She is so angry. She is like the biggest bully in the school. Mary and Allison will have gym together next semester. Mary is hoping that she is on the same team as Allison so that she does not have to compete with her in anything. I can't be*lieve* that you're her friend on Facebook!"

"I feel bad for her," I say. "I'm looking for an opportunity to show her Jesus". I write on her FB wall that Jesus loves her and ask Nicole about what happened. Apparently, Allison got in a fight with another girl at the game. Her explosive outburst caused the police to subdue her before taking her away.

Wow. I wondered what was going on in her home at that very moment.

CHAPTER 6

Epiphany

A few nights ago, I had another strange dream. It took place on the steps that lead to the garage of the house where I grew up. I had not been there for years, and even in my dream, could tell that the house had been unoccupied. "The stairs are the same as always", I thought to myself as I descended into the pit of the garage. I looked around and slowly absorbed what I saw. There were cobwebs all around, and old piles of wood and junk filled the garage. There was this creepy worm-like thing – huge – kind of like a tent worm, but about a million times the size. It was probably about 4 inches in diameter and about a foot long and was mostly white, but with giant bumpy things with whisker-like hairs sticking out of it. It was creeping its way toward me and I was terrified. As I was thinking about what I could use to stave it off, I imagined what would happen if I smashed a bug that big with one of the boards nearby. Gross. Suddenly, out of nowhere, there was this little brownish-black bat-like dog that came out of no-where and attacked me. Its body looked like a little wiener dog, but its head looked like a bat, complete with pointy ears and fangs. Before I knew what had happened, the bat-like creature had bitten me. I was trying to fend it off, so I shoved the palm of my hand into its face and it yelped in pain. The white-worm had changed its direction and was now creeping away from me. It seemed that there was another person there – someone who had either just entered the garage or one who had witnessed the whole thing, I was not sure. Then I woke up. "I have to write this in my dream journal," I thought to myself. I wonder where it is.... I cannot even remember the last time I wrote in my dream journal.

The day that I bought my dream journal to record my "sleep" dreams, I also bought another notebook for the purpose of recording my aspirations and putting on paper the strategic plans to achieve them. I had been doing a lot of thinking about my career, and the decisions that I have made in my lifetime. I have enjoyed a successful engineering career but recognized that my decision to become an engineer instead of a musician lies directly on common sense rather than a process of seeking what God would have me do. Over the years, as I have made job changes, I have learned more to allow God to provide the opportunities for me. He has clearly opened and closed doors throughout my life, making it clear to me that, just as Jeremiah 29:11 indicates - He has a plan for me. I believe he has blessed me with career opportunities within the field that I had chosen, but within the past few years, I had begun to wonder how my career and life would have been different had I truly sought God's will when I decided which career path to take.

I remember the first job change that I made. I had worked for a small company in the East Hills of Framingham for two years since graduating from college with my degree in electrical engineering. The man who owned the company professed a belief in Christ but did not live a life accordingly. He was involved in some business transactions that I felt were shady, and he had created a gossip culture on the production floor of the contract assembly shop that he started. I hated working there and found it difficult to get out of bed in the morning to get ready for work. Week after week, I had perused the classified ads in the Sunday paper, and sent out some resumes, but had not heard anything. After about 3 months of this, my frustration level had elevated so much that I had begun to question my own ability to market my skills. Clear as a bell, I distinctly remember the day that I went to lunch at the Elephant Bar, my job search weighing heavy on my heart. I was trying to understand why God would not provide me with a new opportunity, and I was praying about it while dining alone. In my conversation with Jesus that afternoon, I surrendered my life to Him again as I prayed, "Dear Jesus, I do not understand why I am here in this job that I hate, and why every attempt that I have made to change jobs has been thwarted. Nevertheless, I know that you are always in control and I know that you have a plan for my life. I can only conclude that there is someone here at this company that needs to know you, so I want You to know that if You want me to be here for that purpose, then I willingly surrender my own desires for yours." A tremendous rush of peace flowed through my body as I finished my prayer. I had never experienced a peace like this, but I had never completely trusted God with my decisions before.

What happened later that week would have an effect on my spiritual life forever. On Thursday of that week, I went on a first time sales call to a company in Lowell, MA that was just getting ready to launch a new medical device. The company had existed for a while, but predominantly as a design company. They were just beginning to look at developing the manufacturing process. I had a pleasant enough discussion with the Director of Operations, presenting to him the capabilities of our contract manufacturing shop, looking for new business to bring to the company. As we talked, the conversation turned to what he was looking for as he developed his manufacturing organization. Somehow or another, the topic of my own experience came up. When I mentioned that I had done a college internship working in the Test Engineering department of a gas detector manufacturing company, his interest was piqued. He said he was looking for a manufacturing/test engineer. I provided him with a copy of my resume, and he interviewed me right on the spot and offered me a job before I left.

As I reflected on God's timing of that series of events in my life, what I realized was that it was all about the full surrender of my life to Jesus that God wanted. You see, in the previous 3 months, I was sure that, on my own, I could find a job in my field with my own efforts. Yes, I had prayed about it and asked God to guide me and provide the opportunities, but until that lunch at the Elephant Bar, I had not really surrendered my heart to His will. Since He knows my heart, he knew that I had not fully surrendered to Him. When I was finally able to surrender my will to His will for my life, He knew it. It was in that moment that He then allowed me to have what I desired because it was in His will and not necessarily my own. It was not so much about needing to stay in that job because there was someone to reach there as it was about my own ability to submit to His will.

I had been so excited about learning that spiritual lesson that I shared that experience with many young people over the years. For people who have never experienced complete surrender to God, it was difficult for them to understand. This lesson was one I hoped never to forget.

I went to work at that company, stayed for about two years before moving on to other companies. With each company move, I sought God's will for timing and opportunity. I believe he has blessed the career choices that I had made, but as I mentioned before, I had wondered how my career would have been different if different choices had been made earlier in my life.

Within the past several years as my passion for making a difference in peoples' lives has increased, I have periodically thought about opening a coffee shop. The coffee shop would have a small stage where people could express themselves through music or spoken word.

My vision included creating a place where young people could hang out, developing their artistic abilities. It could be a complete center for the arts – possibly have people who could teach teens how to do dramas, and a recording booth for young bands, and an open space for Friday evening concerts. It could be a venue for all different types of music. It would be awesome to use people that I have met along the way to work there in some capacity – perhaps inexpensive classes offered to the locals, taught by talented young adults looking to develop their own skills of teaching arts, etc. The notebook that I bought with my dream book was bought to develop all of the thoughts around this dream.

I had spent enough time during my day job developing strategic plans and vision and mission statements for the Operations group that I felt I could do a good job creating a business plan. I had even kept my eyes open on new properties as they have become available when businesses folded, etc. There were several buildings right in along the main corridor of our town that would be perfect, I thought.

CHAPTER 7

Camus MA foo

"Mother died today. Or perhaps yesterday, I can't be sure" is one of my favorite lines from a book that I read in high school. Dim hopelessness overshadows the search for significance when we buy into the existential believe that life has no purpose. We disconnect from the reality of the pain we once felt to become oblivious to the pain that surrounds us. This is fallacy. It promotes into being the realization that we are no longer making an impact in our present circumstance. So slippery the slope that before one realizes what happened they find themselves at the bottom of the abyss, desperately searching for the hand that will reach down and pull them to safety. Sometimes the sickness can be so thick that despite being able to recognize it is happening, we are rendered powerless to make a change.

I have lived this fallacy – and it actually works. Six years ago, I made a very conscious decision to stop feeling. It was actually amazing to me how well it worked. I simply shut the feeling off. At the time, I believed that becoming disconnected from the hurt feelings and battered emotions that have betrayed me so many times would enable me to get past the struggles that were bringing me down. The results were tremendous. I was able to ignore the things in my life that were causing me pain. Suddenly, I was able to focus on accomplishing tasks rather than building relationships that were not worth the trouble. Focusing on the tasks that needed to be done suited me well – as a "thinker", not a "feeler" in the Myers-Briggs personality type anyway, I found it extremely favorable to shut off my feelings. When I made the decision, I really had no idea if, or to what degree it would work. However, as time wore on, I found that my mechanical instinct was to solve the problem; and that I did.

I focused on planning activities and becoming involved in doing things. The busier I was, the less interaction with people I had to have. It was great. I loved doing things. At work, I made tremendous differences because I focused on getting things done and not wasting time building relationships. I worked sometimes through the night at the office, coming home only to shower in the morning before heading back in. I was praised for this and received promotions and bonuses as rewards.

At times, Andrew would look at me with wonder. Our relationship had virtually died. Actually, it had died long before my decision to become calloused, but at least I did not grieve anymore. One day he looked at me and asked, "Why is it that you act like you do not care?" I was able to truthfully look him back in the eye and answer coldly, "Because I don't".

Chapter 8

The DA

I had promised Aubrey that I would go with her to the District Attorney's office. I had heard her story. So had the state police. Aubrey had shared it with the detective over a year ago. She said that he had recently contacted her to see if she would come to talk to the DA to see if there was enough of a case to prosecute. I took a half a day vacation from work, picked her up at her job and drove her to the courthouse in Garnerstown. She really did not have anyone functional in her life who would do those kinds of things for her. I did not really want her to have to go through that alone.

She lived with her aunt now – as of last month when she got out of the 28-day drug rehab program into which she had checked herself. Her own home was not healthy. Her dad was an alcoholic. Her brother was a drug user who sometimes coerced her to use drugs against her will. I do not even really remember when exactly I met Aubrey. I remember seeing her at youth group a couple of times… and then she requested me to be her friend on Facebook. When I saw the comments she posted on line, I was worried about her. I asked Pastor Ian one time if he knew her and if he knew she was a wreck. He said that he had talked with her many, many times, and knew she was reaching out for help. He was afraid that one day she would try too hard and accidentally succeed in committing suicide.

The past year had brought so many changes to her life. She came to the first week of Let Go Let God... and the next, and the next... she finished the first program and started again in January when the program started up again, and she finished that program. Now she was posting scripture verses instead of pleas for help. Was that part of the masquerade? I wondered.

So there we were, in the lobby of the district attorney's office. "Hi, are you Aubrey?" a tall, slightly graying man in a suit and tie asked. "Yeah, that's me", she said. I stood up to follow them. "This is really between her and us", the man said to me. "I'm here for her moral support," I quietly replied, and followed the two men into the conference room. She slid into the chair along the same side of the wall as the door. I slid in beside her, closest to the door. "Do not run," he said, kind of laughing and briefly left the room. Where exactly did he think she was going to go, I wondered. She was not the one in trouble here.

A few minutes later, Detective Smith and District Attorney Joe Ramouff entered the room. They each had what appeared to be a copy of the police report and a notepad. Joe said, "Ok, let's start back at the beginning and talk through the events of the evening in question. What is your address?"

"2878 Lincoln Ave", Aubrey replied.

"And the incident took place where?" Joe asked.

"2879 Lincoln Ave, right next door," she replied. Her demeanor was very Matter-of-fact. Her voice did not quiver, though I imagined that she was nervous inside. She answered his questions without hesitation. To me, she seemed to be honest.

"I went next door to hang out with Kathy and Terry".

"How long had you known Kathy and Terry?"

"I knew Terry for about 5 years and Kathy for about 2." She went on to describe the background to the evening in question. Terry had lived next door to her for about 5 years prior to the event. He lived there with his girlfriend. At one point during that time, he had a parole violation and went back to prison for a while. While in prison, his girlfriend moved out – to just a couple doors up the road. Then someone else moved into the house next door – Kathy and her mom. Her mom was a bus driver. Kathy was a hairdresser and a stripper. When Terry got out of prison, he somehow hooked up with Kathy, began to date her, and moved in with her and her mom, back into the same house he used to live in.

"Do you realize how strange that story sounds?" Joe asked. Aubrey responded that she did realize that, but it was the truth. Easton was one of those depressed towns that I had read about in sociology class in college – the kind of towns that generation after generation end up on welfare and cannot seem to pull themselves out of the lot that life had cast them. The soap-opera-like relationships of the people who lived in Easton seemed like they could not possibly be real.

"So it was common for you to go over to Kathy and Terry's?" Joe asked, reviewing his notes.

"Yes, I went over there a lot".

"And what did you do when you were there?" Joe asked.

"Drugs, drinking" was the reply.

"Were you drinking on the night in question?"

"Yes."

"What were you drinking?"

"Beer".

"How much beer did you consume that night?"

"About 9 or 10 beers."

"Was it common for you to drink 10 beers?"

"Yes, I did that frequently." "Did you do any drugs that night?"

"Yes, cocaine."

"In what form?" he asked.

"Rocks and lines," she said.

Therefore, they established that she had been drunk and high and that the next thing she knew Kathy was taking off her shirt and holding her down while Terry was having his way with her. Then she woke up at 5:30 in the morning, and went home to get ready for school. The men seemed to be surprised when they asked if Aubrey's dad said anything to her when he saw her the next morning and she said no. I was sitting there thinking what a wreck her life was. Although I grew up in a single-family home, it was not because of the dysfunction that seemed so to prevail in Aubrey's life. Aubrey's dad had to know these things were going on. How could a father possibly want his daughter to be in a compromised position, sending her over to the neighbor's house knowing that there had been previous drug arrests, parole violations, and strippers?

My mind drifted to what Aubrey's father must be like. I knew very little about him except that he had been married several times, worked as a bartender for extra cash from his regular job in a metal shop. He seemed to be annoyed at the fact that he had a daughter to protect. He knew she was dating a man that was in his 30s and did not see anything wrong with that. I was angry with him; angry that he allowed Aubrey to grow up so dysfunctional; angry that he was so dysfunctional himself. It is the cycle. It can be broken, but it requires someone with inner strength and determination. He is weak, thinking he is powerless to change the cycle that his socioeconomic status has determined for him. He has not met Jesus.

I sat there very quietly, observing the two men as well as Aubrey. I had heard Aubrey's story before, though admittedly not in nearly the same detail. I am sure that nothing surprised the law enforcement people. They have probably heard it all before. I guessed each of them to be in their 40's.

The silvery-gray that appeared around the temples of DA Joe actually did make him look more distinguished. It gave him a seasoned-well-enough appearance to dominate the courtroom. This was probably important to him. Although he did not seem to be arrogant, I thought that he might actually be glad to see some chrome on his head. He wore a ring from Duquesne University. He must have gone to law school there, I thought. Good school. He must be good at what he does.

Detective Smith peered through his glasses. His shoulders

were broad. His shirt was crisp and white – even late on a Friday afternoon. He was dressed nicely, his reddish-brown hair combed neatly.

Both men wore gold wedding rings. I briefly wondered what their family lives were like – did they have children that they worried about every day? I decided that detective Smith probably did have kids, close in age to my own kids.

It did not surprise them when Aubrey told them that it was common for her to drink 10-12 beers and that her dad did not' really care that she did. They did not seem surprised when she told them that Kathy worked as a stripper in a house near Boston, or that she dated a drug dealer that was 37. District Attorney Joe did stop her story long enough to ask if she realized what was wrong about an 18-year-old dating at 37-year-old. She said she did.

After painstakingly retelling her story in more detail than I had heard before, the two men looked at each other and shook their heads. Joe talked first. "My role here isn't to determine if something did or did not happen. My role in all of this is to determine if we can convince a jury of 12 people who do not understand the drug world, that your story is credible. I personally believe that something happened. However, we do not have any physical evidence. We do not have any witnesses willing to step forward. We have a he-said, she said situation. Without any evidence, I cannot make a recommendation to pursue this case."

I had been quiet all this time. I knew this was not what Aubrey wanted to hear, but I understood why he said what he did. If the case ever got to trial, the defense attorney would have a field day making Aubrey look like she had somehow asked for it. I did not just want to drop the situation like that, so I engaged in the conversation and asked what exactly it would take to turn the case. Bottom line... We needed evidence or someone to confess. The police had already talked with Terry – and in fact, he said that he knew something had happened because when they talked, he purposely said that Aubrey was seventeen. After Terry first said that nothing sexual at all happened, he later said, "I thought she was 18!" The problem was that there was no evidence or anyone willing to say that a rape had occurred.

"What about the girl that you said was there at first?"
"Missy"
"What's her last name?"
"Bell. Missy Bell. I used to babysit her kids. She would come over to Kathy's to do drugs, too, but on this night, she had to leave early."

Missy Bell. Wow. I could hardly believe my ears. I had not heard that name in probably 27 years. I had not even thought about Missy since... I could not even remember when. I tried to remember how I even knew Missy. All I remembered was going to visit her at the group home after she had run away from home. She had a troubled home-life. I vaguely remembered that she was born out of wedlock to a girl who was the sister of Mark, who lived across the street from my boyfriend Jeff. I think I was in first grade with Missy. I do not remember her in elementary school – and only vaguely in junior high. It seemed to me that she ran away from home when we were in junior high. She had either flunked a grade or been held back or something – she was no longer in my class in school. Somehow, our paths crossed again. Maybe at church? Who knows? At any rate, I had tried to show her Jesus. I had reached out to her all those years ago, my friendship to bestow, hoping to make a difference in her life. All those years ago. Obviously, my attempts had failed. Epic fail. That is what I would call it now.

I thought about the work that I was doing with Let Go Let God. Would it ever make a difference? Would I ever make a difference? Who was I fooling? It was an epic fail 27 years ago.... and it would be an epic failure now. Why did I even care to make a difference in peoples' lives? I was just fooling myself.

So there I was with Aubrey, failing there, too. We thanked the men for their time. They said that they were glad that it seemed

Aubrey was working on getting her life back in order, recommended that she simply put these bad years behind her, and move on.

When we left, I asked Aubrey how she felt. I was not sure what to expect – I guess I rather expected her to be upset. She was not. She said that she is ready to put it all behind her and move on, just as they had suggested. I told her that I had prayed and asked that God would allow whatever is best for Aubrey to happen. I believed that this was best. Having to live through cross-examination on the witness stand would not have been fun for Aubrey. It was better this way.

I drove Aubrey home to her house. I never mentioned Missy Bell and the connection that we had so many years ago. I was not ready for Aubrey to see my failures for fear of how they would affect her. I just kept up the masquerade.

CHAPTER 9

The End of the Story

The words rang clear in my ears. He must be talking about me, I thought. I sat there in the nakedness of the moment, wondering if anyone else could have known that he was talking to me.

The last time that I heard the message as loudly and clearly as this was when Pastor Charles started his sermon with the very deliberate and direct advice from T.D. Jakes. The message was about knowing when to allow people to walk out of your life. He talked about how sometimes we chase after people as they are walking away – and said we should not chase them. The fact that they are walking away does not make them bad people, it just tells us that their part in our story is over, and we should allow it to be over because we cannot make people stay in our story forever. We have to know when to let it go.

I relived the loss of my friendship with Eileen as if it happened yesterday. My best friend since first grade, she abruptly decided in our sophomore year that we were no longer friends. I had no idea why. One day, she stopped talking to me, never offering an explanation. The loss reincarnated recently because of the loss of my friendship with Rob, with whom I worked, which ended as abruptly as my friendship with Eileen.

I remember the sermon vividly. I had been licking my wounds, wallowing in the excruciating pain inflicted by the best friend I had ever had. I had never heard of TD Jakes before, but could not wait to get home that day to search Google for the message that contained that quote. I wanted to read it again for myself. It was as if God was speaking directly to me through Pastor Charles. It was over. The friendship that I had really come to relish; over, just as unexpected and abrupt as the stop caused by a concrete wall that I felt like I had run into. I just needed to get over it.

I needed to hear those words. I needed to say goodbye to Rob; to grieve the loss of our friendship and move on to recovery. I was actually relieved. I wondered then how my story would end. What would happen to all of the people who had taken part in my story? Would I ever know?

My mind refocused to the present. So here he was, talking about the church growing and starting three services. He said there were some people who were unhappy about this. Well, I was not one of them. I was thrilled that the church was growing. I had been part of a church that grew before, added services and expanded their building. It was exciting to see God working in the lives of the people in growing churches. Then Pastor Charles said something very interesting, and this is what I thought he must have been saying to me. He talked about when friends drop in to visit unexpectedly around dinnertime. Because you value them and you want to continue your friendship, you invite them to stay and dine with you. It might mean that you have to make some room at the table, and perhaps it means that you have a little bit less so that you can give some food to others. My gift of music. He must be asking me to step aside and make room for others to step up and play.

All of a sudden, I began to wonder if, in my desire to honor God, I had overstepped my boundaries. Maybe I should give up my music altogether. It would probably just be better that way – then other people can step up and play. See, that was something else that I messed up. What makes it worse is that I was too stupid to see it.

My mind wrestled with the fact that it seemed to be okay for other people to fulfill their dreams and honor God with their gifts. Why was it not okay for me? The double standard so often permeates our society.

Perhaps God was trying to tell me that it is time to move on to a different place to use my gifts. Maybe I have had all the impact that I am ever going to where I am, and it is just time to move somewhere else. The thought of starting something over did not really excite me. It is hard work, and it would not be fair to the kids. They are just now beginning to blossom in their own lives, learning about the world around them and making their own friends and decisions. To force them to move somewhere else could have a devastating effect on them. No, I did not want to do that now.

I was overwhelmed that Sunday afternoon with the feeling that I should give up music forever.

CHAPTER 10

Dreams and Nightmares

The baby died. Did I even know the baby was born? Oh, yes, I did. I remember now, Maria was pregnant. Prior to the baby, her youngest child was 10 years old. She had just celebrated her 50th birthday – and she had a baby this summer. We all thought she was crazy to have a fourth child. She had a terrific pregnancy – she looked and felt terrific all the way through.

Maria is the mother of Nicole's friend. Nikki and Ashley have been friends since first grade.

Then something happened to the baby after she was born. I remember going to visit her in the home, and I remember having to tell Nicole the news that her best friend's baby sister died.

Then I woke up. I really need to stop having these dreams about people dying. They seem so real when they are happening. I can feel myself crying in them, and feel the heartsick feeling in my stomach when there is absolutely nothing that I can do to change the situation. Why do I dream like that? I have read about cases where people who are on medication or have taken drugs in the past can have "episodes" or influence their dreams, but I am not on medication, nor have ever taken illicit drugs. I hit the snooze bar on my alarm and rolled back over, not ready to get out of bed yet.

Pastor Charles asked me to read aloud from the bulletin. I was not nervous; I had read aloud in large groups many times before. Obediently, I reached my hand out to take the bulletin from his outstretched hand. I looked at the peach-colored half sheet of paper, trying to make sense of the words and numbers in the table on the paper. There was a table of rows and columns on the paper; it actually extended onto the back of the paper, so I had to keep turning it back and forth to see the entire table. Words, spelled phonetically, appeared on one line of the table. Several lines below the phonetically spelled words were more words. Some words were in English, but they did not really seem to make sense. On rows in between, there were numbers and other mathematical symbols, some of which I did not recognize.

There was a small group of people in the room. I slowly recounted the story captured on the rows and columns of the table on the paper. It did not seem to make sense. The words coming out of my mouth did not match the words that were in my head. I have never had this problem before – it was as if I had had a stroke and just could not get my brain to connect with the words that were leaping out of the page. The story began... a couple of times I stopped, desperately hoping that Pastor Charles would see me struggling and put me out of my misery by allowing me to stop and have someone else read. However, he did not. He simply waited for me to finish the anecdote.

The look on his face was not one of disapproval, as I would have thought. Rather it was one of patient encouragement, as if he was saying, "it is ok, you can make it, but you need to be the one to do it – I cannot do it for you-you will see why when you reach the end". A complete sense of failure overwhelmed me and shook my body to its core. I had never before been in such a position where I could not even speak. What was happening to me?

A thousand times before, I have failed. None of my failures felt quite as excruciating as that which I felt in these moments.

It seemed like an eternity of time had passed, as I was still struggling with getting the words to come out of my mouth. Agonizing, I added the numbers. They were fractions.... $5/8 + 7/16 + 1/4$, and so on. I was adding the fractions, some of them less than 1, and some of them more than 1. I added them in my head, it clicked that in the mathematical equation, there would be 1 left over... and I had that eureka moment where all of the nonsense in the story came together at the end to make the point that I needed to hear. The answer to the riddle in the anecdote was that Jesus always has one more left over for us. Suddenly, I understood why Pastor Charles allowed me to struggle the whole way through the story – to force me to get to the end and see the result for myself.

What did this dream mean? One more what? I knew that the anecdote was trying to point out that no matter how much we need, Jesus ALWAYS has enough to give. As humans, we do not have unlimited energy – we get tired and frustrated and unable to give more. We can see this with people who are caregivers to people with special needs – a sometimes-thankless job, with rewards seemingly only in Heaven. In our humanness, we are limited; but in his Holiness, He has always got more to give. Finally, after all of the months of nonsense dreams that made no sense to me, I had an answer to one. I was suitably jubilant to accept the meaning of this particular dream at face value, and the hope that it represented.

At 4:30 AM, I awakened suddenly by the sound of the telephone. Groggily, I stumbled out of my bed and over to the phone. "Uh, Charissa?" "Yeah," I said, my eyes still adjusting to the light that I turned on by the bed. The voice on the other end was a familiar one. It was John Burns. He is the co-leader of Let Go Let God. His voice was slow and deliberate. "Uh... I just wanted to call and tell you myself. We just got word that Sam is dead. Looks like suicide."

The words hit me like a ton of bricks. Sam had come to the very first class of Let Go Let God. Her mother and father were pillars in the church, and taught Sunday school, Vacation Bible School and led small group Bible studies in their home. Their daughters were beautiful. They had attended the finest Christian school in the area. The oldest had graduated several years ago and gone on to school to become a missionary. She was currently serving in a remote location of Tanzania. But in her senior year of high school, Sam had become friends with the 30 something neighbor who introduced her to a different lifestyle – one that included sex, drugs, and rock n' roll. The more Sam's parents protested, the more it drove Sam to her neighbor's house. Sam was desperately looking for a way to meet what she felt her parents' expectations were of her – and was always falling short. Eventually, she stopped trying; and then rebelled against them. There was no point in trying if she knew she'd always fail.

Sam tried everything to hurt her parents. She began to smoke, first cigarettes, and then weed. She was promiscuous and drank regularly. She graduated from high school and began to attend the local community college, but was on academic probation because she failed three of four classes in her first semester.

I remembered the first day she came to LGLG. She sat rebelliously in the back row, sneering periodically through the large group session, rolling her eyes as the leaders talked about the need to get help. When it came time to break into small groups, she said she really was not interested, but followed the leaders into the room anyway. For the next several weeks, Shari and I tried our best to establish a relationship of trust with Sam. She came back every week but insisted that she did not need to get help. We asked her why she kept coming back; she insisted that it was because of her parents; however, Sam was, by this time, 20 years old. Although she was living in their house, for all practical purposes was out on her own. She had made it clear to them and to everyone around that they could no longer tell her what to do. Yet, every week she showed up, claiming that they were making her come.

I was new as a sponsor during this session, but what I felt was that she really did want help, but wanted to pretend that she was this hard-core tough girl who did not need anyone's help. She never did get to the point where she admitted she needed help. She was simply living her life dangerously, moving from guy to guy, friend to friend, acting as if she did not really care about anyone or anything. Even to the very last session, she insisted she didn't need anything from anyone.

Wow. Now she was dead. I failed again. I failed to reach her – failed to help her see that she did not need to live a life of pretense – that Jesus would love her as she was. What I suspected happened was that she had made a bad choice at some point in her life – perhaps it was trying drugs, perhaps it was giving herself to a person that she thought loved her – who knows. I felt like she could never forgive herself and so she built this tough outer shell around herself so that no one could see her pain. The Masquerade. It is all around us.

I hung up the phone and turned the light back off. I sat there in the darkness of my bedroom for hours, staring into the abyss of my own mind, trying to make sense of what drove Sam to the final curtain call. Oh, how my heart ached right now. So much that it actually made me sick to my stomach. I had failed her parents. I had failed myself. I had just failed.

The anguish I felt ate away at me – I was angry for the failures that I have had. What made me think that I could change the world? I mean, Satan is so much bigger than I am. I am nothing. Worth nothing. Why did I ever try to change Sam? I should give up, just as she did.

My thoughts turned back to my own hopelessness. I, too, was unable to forgive myself for the deepest darkest secret that I have never told. I thought that by helping other people deal with their forgiveness issues, I could experience forgiveness vicariously through them. I was wrong. Dead wrong. I should probably just end my misery, too, I thought as I lay in the darkness.

I thought back to the song that I had written when I was about 15 years old – the words were still so true today – and it exemplified my life. How prophetic the words were when I wrote them – who knew…

I Cried Out

I walked alone in darkness, along a dark pathway.
I walked along in silence, had nothing left to say.
Ahead I saw a figure – could not make out its form
Its state in total agony – a hopeless soul, forlorn.

Sitting there on the edge of despair
I wanted to help, to show that I cared
I heard strange noise escaping, deep from its inner self
like the sounds of souls who lament within the depths of Hell

I cried out for someone
To come and answer me
To heal my broken heart
And set me free

Each cry came out more feeble, more desperate than the last;
And still each cry, unanswered, went off into the past
I reached out my hand, my friendship to bestow;
And as I reached I realized what I had not yet known.

This poor soul who was sitting and crying all alone
Turned out to be the same soul – none other than my own.

I thought about all of the hopeless souls to whom I had reached out – my friendship to bestow…. They were still hopeless despite my attempts. Missy Bell – I had tried to help her over 25 years ago now. I had hoped that she would be able to rise above the challenges given her by her life's circumstances. I had shared the story of Jesus with her all those years ago, but it seemed to have no impact. She had thrown her life away, and perpetuated the cycle into the next generation, creating a life for her children similar to the one with which she was so familiar. An unwed mother, struggling to make ends meet, lying to her babysitter, and making drug deals in front of her children. Sam, who had thrown her body and her life away – for what? Lindsay – whatever happened to her? Would I ever know?

Why do I do this to myself? Why do I even care about people? All they do is disappoint me, and all I do is disappoint them.

CHAPTER 11

Judas

Since his email making it perfectly clear where he stood, I tried to stay out of Rob's way at work. I knew his reputation and now had evidence that when he wants to, his bite can be worse than his bark. I remembered a message from T.D. Jakes that Pastor Charles shared in a sermon at church that Sunday. As I reflected his words, I realized I just needed to let his friendship go because his part in my story was over.

At first, my heart was so broken; I did not think I would be able to go on. I felt so betrayed.

That Lenten season, Pastor Dwayne had asked me to come and share music at his church. So on a Saturday evening, I drove out to see them and share their evening worship service with them. I played a few of the Easter pieces that I had arranged for my annual Lenten Service. Pastor Dwayne gave the evening message – he spoke about Judas' betrayal of Jesus – and talked about how Jesus might have felt. It could not have been a more appropriate message for me to hear at that time. I knew exactly how betrayal felt. Brokenhearted, I clung to every word that Pastor Dwayne shared that evening, still trying to find meaning in the pain inflicted by my friend. That evening, I went home and wrote a new song:

Did Jesus Feel Like this?

Beaten and Bruised
Battered and worn
My heart feels so weary,
Tattered and Torn

Betrayed by a friend
It cuts like a knife
Withered and worn,
My soul dies inside

Did Jesus feel like this?
When He felt the Judas kiss?
And did His heart ache inside forevermore?
And could He have cried
When Peter thrice denied?
It's a hurt that can never be restored.

Anguish and torment,
Hopeless despair
Inflicted by one
Who was supposed to care

Desperately, I cried.
Incredible pain
Overwhelming my senses
Pouring like rain.

Did Jesus feel like this?
When He felt the Judas kiss?
And did His heart ache inside forevermore?
And could He have cried

When Peter thrice denied?
It's a hurt that can never be restored.

Stricken with sorrow
Even unto death
My Lord knows our feeling,
He knows them best.

Yes, Jesus felt like this
When he felt the Judas kiss.
And His heart ached inside forevermore
And yes, He could have cried
When Peter thrice denied
It's a hurt that only God restores

CHAPTER 12

Emma

I had been working with Emma for about 3 months in Let Go Let God but knew her for a couple years prior. She came to our youth group. She was a pretty girl with beautiful, blue eyes. I had never seen her smile. Her story was almost unimaginable – a story of abuse that started with a foster parent when she was just 3 years old. At the age of 13, she was addicted to pornography and brought into juvenile detention for sending pornographic photos of herself to a 34-year-old man. She had just begun to open up to me and share some of the things that she had been through in her short life. She had every reason to want to end her life. Her mother, a teenage, unwed mother, had abandoned her on the side of the road shortly after birth. A passer-by found her and brought her to the police. Eventually, she became a ward of the state, placed into foster care. She blocked her earliest memories of foster care. Her therapist told her that was her body's way of healing from the pain. Eventually, through hypnosis, her therapist uncovered that she had been sexually abused, and prostituted by her foster mother. She had spent her first 11 years moving from one foster family to another and eventually placed in a group home called Jacob's Pride. She threatened to stab her teacher in the eye, so the school expelled her. The principal did not know what to do with her. Her latest foster family, Joanne and Matthew Bodinski, were born-again believers. They felt God called them to intervene in the lives of troubled kids. Emma was definitely troubled.

Emma came to live with the Bodinski's about two years ago when she was sixteen. It had not been an easy transition for her or for them. They really seemed to care about her. She had never experienced a caring family and did not know how to respond. She did what came naturally to her; she rebelled... She broke every rule that they laid out for her and said unimaginable things to them. They were so patient with her and showed her much compassion, but tough love. They told her that she needed to make some changes in her life. They had heard about this program, Let Go Let God from their neighbor, who was a teacher in the neighboring school district where Pastor Ian had been working with administrators to encourage troubled teens to be mandated to attend. The school had seen an amazing revival among the students – to where those who had been the biggest troublemakers were now actually leading Bible studies and prayer groups.

I remembered the first night that Emma came in. She did not talk to anyone, just sat quietly in the chair at the far right of the last row. We were on Step 3 – Take Action. In our large group session, we talked about how we needed to take an action step to give over to Christ.

Emma was very frank about the fact that she was not even sure that God existed. Knowing what she had been through in her life, it was no wonder she felt that way; however, I hoped and prayed that by the end of the 16-week LGLG session, she might feel differently.

Being able to face Emma would be difficult this evening. I had to wonder myself, sometimes, where God was in all of this. He sometimes seemed so far away.

I wiped the tears from my face as I hung the towel on the shower door. It was time to get up and put on the masquerade so that people would not be able to see the excruciating pain I was suffering from the loss of Sam. I was not only grieving for her, but for myself, and the failure that this represented. I wanted to show strength in the face of adversity, especially for my children, who were at such an impressionable age themselves. I wanted so badly for them to grow up with a rock-solid faith in Jesus. I wanted to spare them from experiencing the doubt and vulnerability that I had experienced. On some days it is harder to maintain the masquerade. This was one of them.

Chapter 13

Drinking From a Saucer

The cold, December rain pelted us on the head as we ran through the parking lot of Mick's Diner, headed to our weekly breakfast time that I had grown to love. The tradition started a few years ago when Nicole had band practice before school on Tuesdays and Thursdays. Since they both rode the same bus, it seemed to make sense to drive them both to school early. David planned to sit in the lobby of the school until the bell rang for homeroom. As we pulled into the school parking lot, I had an idea to take him out for breakfast instead. That began the monthly tradition of spending a special breakfast time with each of my kids – just "mommy and me" time. Taking turns so that no one felt left out, we would make the ½-mile trek from the school to Mick's Diner and sit at the counter with the swivel chairs having breakfast and sharing whatever was on our minds.

Little did I realize how much those breakfast meetings would change our lives?

"Good morning! How are you today?" we would be greeted by the friendly server. Over the months, we have gotten to know the people who regularly dined at Mick's. Once a month, a church youth group met for a prayer breakfast. Bob McKenzie must dine here every morning. Bob was one of the developers who worked in the area. I knew this from the conversation he had one morning with another patron about the business owner who had just rented the space in the strip mall where the Tasty Cone had been. They were talking about how much the rent was in the space and doubting that his new ice cream business would be profitable enough to stay in business any longer than the Tasty Cone had.

One morning as we entered, an older man was sitting at the counter to our left. We had not seen him before, but he was sitting right near the place where Bob McKenzie usually sits. "I'm drinking from my saucer!" was his response when I asked him how he was. "Do you know what that means?" he asked. Without waiting for a reply, he answered, "It means my cup runneth over with blessing! Do you know what the greatest gift ever was given was?" This time, I answered him before he could. "Absolutely! It was Jesus!" I responded. He looked at me and said, "Do you know, I've been asking people that for 20 years and you are the only person who has ever answered that question. I use that line as a way to tell people about my Lord and Savior. Usually, people just look at me like I'm crazy." I thought to myself that he did seem a little eccentric, but it put a smile on my face to see how unabashed he was about sharing the gospel. There was nothing fancy about him – he had on a faded pair of blue jeans and a shirt that said nothing special. His face was round and jubilant; his hair white as snow. He rather reminded me of my grandfather, who spent time visiting nursing homes to share Jesus with the people who were closing in on meeting their maker. I wondered if he was a traveler passing through town, sharing his joy wherever he went.

Just as the diner door opened and Bob McKenzie entered, the man's phone rang. I had not expected that this vagrant-looking fellow either would have a cell phone or be receiving a phone call at 7:30 in the morning. I laughed silently to myself as I prepared to hear a comical one-sided exchange of words, perhaps with his wife – I fully expected him to kid around with his caller. Ironically, however, he answered his phone with the serious tone of a professional businessperson, and as Bob shook his hand before sitting next to him, I quickly ascertained that he was not a vagrant at all, but probably one of Pleasantville's business owners or land developers. The exchange of words on his cell phone indicated a meeting that was happening later today. Throughout the entire short conversation, the "vagrant's" matter-of-fact tone told me that he was an important man. As he hung up his phone and began to talk to Bob about a project they were working on together, I remember thinking about how different this man acted when it was all about business. I wondered if he had ever tried to make an impact for Jesus during his daily business. I paid our bill and David and I departed for school, wondering if I would see this man again. "Would not it be ironic if... Nah... that would never happen", I thought as I closed the diner door behind me.

CHAPTER 14

Preparing for News

That night as I cleaned up the dishes from dinner and kissed the kids goodnight, I thought about Emma. I feared that she would see failure written all over my face when the news of Sam broke tonight. I knew that I would not be the only one devastated by the news – that all of the adult workers would feel the same. We knew the reality when we began a ministry that not every person would come to faith in Jesus. People coming through the program would have to choose for himself or herself whether they would accept the gift, just as all of humanity must choose. Some people never do. In those people, we experience a small glimpse of the disappointment that God must feel when the people that he created to love Him turn their backs. The pain pierces my chest and my heart bleeds. I can only imagine how God feels.

The mood of the social time was particularly somber tonight. John called all of the adult leaders to prepare them for the news that he would break to the students tonight. I could tell that some of the sponsors had been crying. As the social time approached its end and John asked if we could all take our seats, I sat next to Emma.

"It is with deep sorrow and regret that we open tonight by sharing some news that I had hoped never to have to share with any of you," John slowly began. "Last night, we lost one of our own.

Some of you know Sam Smith. Sam took her own life last night." A hushed gasp fell over the room from the people who had not yet heard the news. "You know, sometimes we try to help people, and we all want to see people get healthy... and then something like this happens, and we wonder where have we failed. Satan will use moments like these to challenge each of you in this room – the sponsors and the kids – to make you feel like you are failing and you really should not even try. Do not let Satan win. I have been a professional counselor for many years, and know that we lose some of the battles. It hurts. It will make you think that you should give up fighting.... I want to encourage all of you tonight not to give up. If you need to talk about anything, you can call me anytime. As counselors and sponsors, and students, we need to have a support network – to lift each other up in prayer - and to be able to share when we're feeling down so that Satan does not defeat us."

How did John know what I was feeling at that moment? Were the other sponsors feeling that way, too? Perhaps it was normal to feel that way. At this moment, I wanted nothing more than to go home and hold my kids tight. I knew that I had to be strong for Emma and the others, though, despite feeling like the biggest failure imaginable. I took a deep breath before heading to our small group session, not sure what to expect.

That night in our small group, Emma promised she'd never commit suicide. Ironically, she said that she was seriously considering suicide just days before – she had planned the whole thing out – she had been mutilating herself for so long, that people would think she just took it too far. She was going to cut her wrists in the bathtub. However, something told her to come one more time to Let Go Let God. I knew that it was the Holy Spirit urging her to try just one last time to feel Him. She thought about the words that her foster dad had told her when she called him to say good-bye. He told her that it would be the last night she felt that way. He asked her to look him in the eyes so that he knew that she knew what he was telling her – he told her that Jesus would wrap her in His arms and never let her go. It was then that Emma's heart began to soften, and God began to work a miracle in her life.

For me, this night was excruciating. Though Sam was no longer in my small group, I could not help but feel that I could have done something; should have done something different. I felt the same way when Morgan died, responsible. Actually, if I was honest with myself, I felt responsible when my dad died, too. Though I was only eight years old and the youngest daughter, I remember an overwhelming sense that I was now responsible for my family. Perhaps that was the real reason why I became an engineer. Maybe I was just fooling myself. This whole thing with Sam was more than enough reason for me to give up trying to help people. I had been on a four-month battle with depression as it was, and this was the proof that I needed that I had been fooling myself all along and just did not realize it. For me, this would be the end of the road, a goodbye of sorts – a goodbye to trying to help people.

CHAPTER 15

The Gift

The months following the death of my friendship with Rob wore on, and my heart began to heal from its injuries. I found new meaning for my life through my sponsorship of Let Go Let God. I witnessed God making a difference in people's lives, including my own. I had rededicated my own life to Christ, and made a commitment to Him to be "all there". During this time of pain, I grew spiritually; so much so that I wondered what had ever taken me so long to surrender to Christ. My relationship with Jesus continued to grow, and my wounded heart healed by developing more compassion for others who still need to know Him.

At work, I focused on completing what I needed. I avoided attending meetings where I thought Rob would attend. One of the projects I worked on was a product releasing from the group in which Rob worked. There were times when we needed to communicate with each other. I was extremely careful to preface any communications with Rob about the project and keep focus strictly on business.

One evening, I learned of a problem with a particular product. I knew that I needed to let Rob know about the problem, but I really did not want to. Slowly, I mustered up the courage to type the email regarding the issue. His response came back quickly, more quickly than I would have expected due to the evening hours. He said,

"Thank you for letting me know about this, Charissa. We will have a team working on resolving it starting first thing in the morning. PS. You are still my friend".

What? What could that possibly mean? Friends do not betray each other's trust. He had made it perfectly clear months before that we were no longer friends and here, he was telling me that we were still friends.

What I wanted so badly at that moment was the reconciliation of our friendship. I realized that it would never be the same, but I wanted desperately to understand what made Rob act the way that he did. There I sat, in the room dimly lit by the light from my computer, responding to him that I was sorry our friendship had ended. His response to me was, "you know my heart. You know how I think. No need to say Sorry, I see it in your eyes every time we speak."

I thought back to the email where Rob had said he thought we were "fate mates". It was indeed strange – the connection that we had felt. It was obvious from his statement that he felt it too. It was definitely unmistakable, but I really did not understand what it meant. Losing that connection was like having an umbilical cord severed. I did not know if I had ever bought into the "fate mate" philosophy, but I badly wanted reconciliation. I had been praying about it so much since we had started a new Sunday school class on conflict management. Did I know his heart? No, I did not know his heart.

Over the next several weeks, I cautiously approached conversations with him. The project he was working on required my group's involvement, so there were some opportunities to attend meetings with him. In these meetings, he seemed to be friendly enough, though the sting of his beating was still fresh in my mind. One day, I mustered up enough courage to ask him if we could meet to talk. I had prepared my speech carefully and methodically. I wanted to ask him why he did what he did. I wanted him to know how badly he had hurt me, but how God had used that pain to grow my relationship with Him.

The morning we were to meet was a few days before Christmas. I brought a thermos of coffee to break the ice. With some trepidation, I broached the subject of his betrayal. When I asked him why he would have shared my personal information with his wife, Cass, he could not answer. He said that Cass had accused him of having an affair and he wanted to prove to her that we were not. I told him that the entire situation reminded me of Joseph and his brothers – and I read for him the scripture in Genesis 50:20 "You intended to harm me, but God intended it for good to accomplish what is now being done, the saving of many lives".

With that, Rob said that he was truly sorry for hurting me, and embraced me in forgiveness. It was only the second time I had ever had any physical contact with him. "Thank you, Jesus, "I whispered to myself as he walked away. I had asked Him to provide reconciliation, and this was a reconciliation of sorts – I would take it, glad to have had the opportunity to show him that what resulted from my pain was a stronger faith in Jesus.

That evening, I sat down at my piano and wrote another song. I called it, "I'm Going Home"

I'm Going Home

I'm going home
I don't know when
But I can't wait until
I can live again
I am so worn

And the music fades into the night
Give me your Light
Make everything right
Give me your Light

Mistakes….
I've made a few
But You give the strength I need to make it through
I'm so glad

And the music fades into the night
Give me your Light
Make everything right
Give me your Light

But I lost my way
And You found me filled with despair
But you didn't leave me
You came to save me and show me that you care

I'm Going Home
I don't know when
But I will see you when I get to Heaven, Friend

I am so worn

And the music fades into the night
Give me your Light
Make everything right
Give me your Light

CHAPTER 16

Knives, Forks, and Blades

Several months after Allison's arrest, she wrote on my Facebook wall, "Charissa, I love you. I have started going to church" I wrote back, excited to learn that someone from her school had taken an interest in her and was taking her to church each week. We conversed a bit and she said she would still like to meet for coffee sometime. I asked her if she would like to go out to lunch that Sunday after church. She asked me if I minded picking her up at her church.

"You're NOT bringing her to our house, are you mom?" my daughter asked. She and her friends were still somewhat afraid of the reputation Blade had earned at school. "You ARE going to meet her in a public place, right? I hope you do not die." I could see she was genuinely concerned. "No, honey, I'm not going to die. I'm meeting a 14-year-old girl for lunch, and I'm taking Jesus with me," I replied. "You know why she acts the way she acts?" Nicole asked. "No, why?" " Her mother committed suicide," Nicole said.

Wow. Instantly, I choked up. I knew that I had the feeling in my heart from the first time Blade had reached out to me that there was a tragedy in her life. I could not explain how or why I felt that way, but somehow I knew that she was looking for a way to deal with grief. From the moment I saw her friend request on Facebook,

I felt as if God had led her to me. It reminded me of the time God led a dog to my home. This subtle reminder showed me that God is, indeed, in control.

My mind thought back to that period, about six weeks before my wedding. It was the day before Easter Sunday, and we were planning to have Easter dinner at my mom's house. Andrew and I were preparing for the details of our wedding, and considering where we would live after we were married. We decided to rent a tiny apartment from friends of ours. I was out running some errands in the morning, and passed a yellow Labrador Retriever on my way back home, about a mile from my house. I do not know why I thought about it, but as I looked at the dog, it occurred to me that he looked like he was lost. He was meandering in the opposite direction of my car, headed toward a gas station near the highway at the end of our residential plan. Quickly and simply, I said a prayer that God would lead this lost dog to its home and continued driving to my own home.

About two hours later, my sister, who had also been running errands, returned home. "Hey, there's a dog laying in the yard under our tree," she said as she entered the door. I had been in the kitchen preparing food for Easter dinner. When I looked out the front door and say the beautiful yellow lab lying in the front yard as if he belonged there, I knew instantly that God had indeed led him to his home.

We wondered how we could manage a third dog, but for the moment, we welcomed "Sebastian" into our home. Surprisingly, he got along quite well with our other two dogs. For the next six weeks, Sebastian graced our lives with his gentleness. We cared for him with food and water and took him to the vet to have him checked over. We had called the police and local veterinarians to see if he belonged to anyone who had reported him missing, but no one had. We fell in love with him immediately, but knew we could not move him to our apartment.

About a month later, one afternoon our neighbor, David, came over to visit. He mentioned that he had seen a "Lost Dog" poster on a telephone pole down the street. The owner had been looking for him since he had gotten away. We were fond of Sebastian and were heartbroken to learn that his name was actually "Rebel". Our hearts were broken even more when Rebels' owner came to pick him up and Rebel had resisted leaving with him. We were not sure what kind of home Rebel had, but from the disheveled appearance of his owner, the alcohol on his breath, and the way that Rebel resisted, we were sure it was not a good one. Rebel took a piece of my heart with him when he left that day, and as I clung to the promise that I knew God had brought him to us for a reason, I prayed that God would keep watch over Rebel.

As my mind returned to Allison's home life, I imagined an abusive situation, perhaps with parents who just did not care. I imagined all sorts of things, but I never imagined that her mother had committed suicide. Given how prevalent the topic had been in my life this fall, I could hardly speak at this moment. "Boy, I'm glad you told me that today so that I could have some time to digest it before I meet with Allison tomorrow". Wow. Suicide. It was everywhere. I wondered just how many individual people know someone who committed suicide – and wondered about the effect of those suicides on everyone around them. I doubted whether the suicide victims themselves ever truly understood the impact of their decisions on the people left behind.

That morning, I could hardly contain myself through the church service as I was wondering what our lunch conversation would be like. I left my church, headed for her church to pick her up. She had mentioned that she would be waiting for me in the grass, but the rain had started this morning. In my initial drive by the front door of her church, I did not see her; I began to wonder if we had gotten signals crossed. I did not have her cell phone number – most of our contact had been through Facebook. I stopped briefly to pray, "Dear Jesus, this meeting is for your glory. I believe that you have arranged this, I just ask you now to help us find each other."

Just then, I pulled back up to the front door and recognized the girl that I had only seen in Facebook pictures. I opened the passenger side door and said, "Are you, Allison? Hi, I'm Charissa." She got into the car with no trepidation at all. Our ride to the restaurant was only a few miles. She immediately seemed to be comfortable with me and began to share with me information about her life.

She mentioned that her mother had passed away 4 years ago. "Was she sick?" I asked. "Well, she was mentally sick. She committed suicide." "Wow. I am sorry. That must have been tough. I lost my dad when I was young, too, to cancer, so I know a little bit about how it feels." We went on to have a delightful lunch, each sharing with each other things that we had gone through. I found her to be very mature. I asked her many questions about her family, trying to ascertain how involved her dad was in her life. She shared with me that she started going to church and really LOVED it – and was hoping to influence her dad and sister to start to come to church.

I thought about how cool it would be for the people at her school who were already afraid of her to see the change that Jesus could make in her life. It could be the start of a revival – and hundreds of kids might come to know Jesus in the process – that would be an answer to prayer for the school district. She could become an Ambassador for Christ. When I mentioned it to her, she said, "I am praying that God uses me that way".

Really? I wondered. Is that part of a masquerade since she knows that I love Jesus? On the other hand, is she genuine...?

CHAPTER 17

Lucy

Sometimes in the evening when I would enter the bedroom, I would see that Andrew was watching a Christian TV station. I knew that in his head, he had many questions about God, but a genuine interest in learning more. He had grown up in a Catholic family, and attended St. John the Baptist parochial school until 9th grade when he met me. I was crazy about him from the first time I laid eyes on him – they were a beautiful light shade of blue and looked as if they could see right through me.

His eyelashes were the longest I had ever seen, much prettier than my own, which I had plucked out the year after my dad died. They grew back over years – the doctor said it was a strange way for me to deal with my fathers' death. I believe it was a form of self-mutilation but took place in an uncontrollable need to pull out an "itchy" eyelash.

I remember the day that my girlfriend, Lynn, had mentioned meeting someone that lived on my street; she wondered if I might be able to fix them up. She described his eyes and eyelashes and then said his name. Instantly, I was green with envy. I had wanted to date him. In addition, Lynn was cute; he would surely be interested in her. I told her that I would try my best, but did not really mean it. I approached him on the bus that afternoon and mentioned to him that I knew someone who was interested in him. "Oh, yeah?" he said with piqued interest. I did not try very hard to fix him up with Lynn. However, I did secure a first date for myself. Years later, as Lynn and I shared dinner together, she laughed as I recounted the story. For all those years I had worried that she would resent me for it, she simply laughed and said she did not even remember it happening. Lynn was married now to a wonderful man who simply adored her. They had two beautiful children, and life for them was good.

My first date with Andrew was memorable. He came to pick me up in his 1977 Camaro. My mom was so excited that I was dating someone other than Jeff. He nervously asked me what kind of music I liked. "Music? I am a musician... I like ALL music," was my reply. "Great. How about country music?" he said. My heart sank. I thought I really did like all kinds of music. But country? I was not sure I considered that music. "Sure, "I said, not wanting to make a bad impression. I kept up that masquerade for several years, even attending a few country music concerts until I finally confessed that I did not like it. Ironically, my kids love country music.

We dated for the remainder of high school. He was a couple of years older than I was and went to work at a local mechanic shop when he graduated. We dated exclusively throughout high school and college – I was crazy about him, and eagerly gave myself to him with the first opportunity I had. He seemed to be very nervous about it the first time. I had lost my virginity to a previous boyfriend and felt that it no longer mattered. He was awkward and nervous the whole time. Within time, however, there was no longer awkwardness, only eagerness to please each other.

Our relationship was good, both physically and emotionally. During the early years, he was very tender and caring – his eyes would light up when he saw me, and I could tell that he was as crazy about me as I was of him. We shared many things together – our hopes, dreams, lamentations, and sins. Eventually, after dating for nine years through high school, college, and early career days, he asked me to marry him. Throughout those 9 years, we had accumulated much baggage, and I felt responsible for his spiritual life. When we were married in 1995, I anticipated a life filled with love and caring, like the life that I had seen modeled in my own parents until my father's death.

Our life together, though, would not be at all the way I pictured it would be. Within the first year of marriage, there were three separate occasions where I packed my things, determined that I had made the biggest mistake of my life. For him, it seemed that his priority was working on other people's cars outside of his normal work hours, or spending time in the garage of our property owner, who was also our friend. Our property owner was an alcoholic, and I worried that the influence would be bad for Andrew. My fears we validated as, night after night, he would come home drunk.

Several years went by, and we bought our first home, had two children, and invited my mom to live with us. Though there were good times, too, my heart ached to feel the love and acceptance that I had seen modeled in my parents' marriage... It simply did not exist in mine. I recalled, with sadness, the times when he treated me nasty in front of other people. I saw the way that other husbands treated their wives at times, gently patting their hand or hugging them in public, proud of the relationships that they had. I longed for that in my own home.

I tried many times to begin to build the relationship that I wanted. I invited him to do couples' devotional books. He always refused, saying that we did not need to do anything like that because our marriage was fine.

There were times where I felt completely overwhelmed by the responsibilities of parenthood, which, for me, for all practical purposes, was like a single-parent family. Many times, I would retreat to the bowels of our basement and contemplate suicide. During those times, the only thing that kept me from doing it was the effect that I knew it would have on my children. I thought about Morgan's children, and wondered what they were doing – had they been able to grow up and be functioning members of society? Did they bear the burden caused by the fact that the one person who was supposed to be a rock-solid role model for them had abandoned them forever in a selfish act of suicide?

During the times that I was feeling particularly lonely, I would role-play in my mind what the reaction might be as people that I knew found out that I had committed suicide. Would they be shocked? Would they care? Would Andrew wish that he had treated me differently? Would people wish that they had known me better, or wish that they had said something to make me feel the love that I so desperately needed?

In the back of my mind, I also knew it was a sin to take one's own life. I still had my faith in Jesus, but He just seemed to be so far away from me. At this point in my life, it was not my faith in Jesus that kept me from suicide. It was my kids. I knew how it felt to lose a parent, and I did not want my children to have to feel that way.

My decision to stop feeling several years ago was surprisingly easy. Out of desperation, after a particular spell of nasty behavior from my husband, I decided not to care anymore. I hardened my heart to be calloused to the pain that he inflicted and mechanically went through life, grasping for meaning in it wherever I could find.

It was so easy not to care anymore. I honestly did not care if he lived or died – in fact, I actually prayed and asked Jesus to take his life. I knew that I could be there for my children just as my mother had been there for me, and I did not need nor want him anymore. I knew that divorce was wrong in God's eyes, so I decided to just live my life and exist in the house together. It would be years before God would soften my heart and give me back a desire to be a true wife to my husband.

As the time wore on, I went about my daily life, as involved as ever in my kids' lives to make up for the void left by the fact that their father was not involved. I desperately wanted him to love them and me. He drank regularly. I actually encouraged his drinking because Andrew was only nice to me when he was drinking. I drank occasionally as well, though mostly just at social events. There were times, however, when I would think about how my life could have been that I would pour myself a strong rum and coke, or two, or three, or four, just to forget what my life was like.

I had started a new job shortly after my decision to stop feeling. I poured myself into my work and became successful. I met a new friend, Laura, whose life turned out to be surprisingly similar to mine. She and I became friends instantly, and I still count her among the best friends I ever had.

One day, Laura shared with me that she and her husband were going to divorce. She just could not take his drinking and abuse anymore. After the divorce, Laura bought a small house, still within the same school district, not far from where we lived. She was having a housewarming bonfire party and invited us to come. I had become so accustomed to attending things alone, like a single parent, that I was flabbergasted when Andrew said he would like to come along. He had always liked Laura, too. I wondered secretly if he had ever wondered what it would be like to kiss Laura, but it never really bothered me.

We showed up for Laura's party early. Many of my work friends were there, including the plant manager and his wife. We all started drinking and eating and having a good time. At one point in the night, the plant manager leaned over to me and said, "Better be careful. Do not forget you just interviewed for a management position on my staff." I did not know him well but felt like I knew him well enough that I could respond to him by saying, "Hey, that's ok. If I am a good fit for the job, then I am, regardless of what happens here. If I'm not, I'm not, regardless of what happens here". Several weeks later, he offered me the position.

I had a great time at the party. Andrew seemed to interact with my friends much better than I had seen in the past, and he and I threw joking jabs at each other throughout the night. I knew that I drank far more than I should have, and as I handed him the keys to drive home later that night, I said to him, "Thank you for actually being nice to me tonight." It meant a lot to me to have Andrew treat me with respect in front of my friend. So many times in the past, he had verbally put me down in front of family and friends that I had very little self-confidence left.

The following week at work, I went on two business trips, both of them with people that had been at the party the weekend before. The first was a driving trip to New Hampshire. We left early in the morning; Brian came to our house to pick me up. Brian had always seemed to like me; we had hit it off well almost as soon as I had started there. As we drove, we talked mostly about business, but a little bit about his wife, whom he adored. She was much older than he was, and had suffered through bad relationships prior. Her kids were almost as old as he was. We drove to our supplier and conducted the business that we needed to, and turned around to come home, all on the same day.

As the time reached 3:30, I knew the kids would be getting home from school, so I called home to see how their day was. After a few moments of talking with them, excited about what they had done, I hung up the phone. Brian said, "I love the way that you interact with your kids. It is so nice to see how excited you get about the things that they do."

"Well, they are my world," I replied.

"You know, there's been something that I've been wanting to talk to you about, but just did not really know how to bring it up. You know that I care a lot about you."

"Yes," I said, slowly, trying to anticipate what would come next. I never expected what he was going to say.

"Why do you let him treat you like that?" he said.

Wow. "Like what?" I asked. I remembered the party the weekend before, and my thanking him for actually being nice to me.

"My stepdaughter was in an abusive relationship; she had to get a protection from abuse order to keep her husband from beating her. At the party last weekend, I watched the way Andrew treated you, and it reminded me so much of how Joe treated Emily. I just can't understand how you can command so much respect at work but allow him to treat you like he does."

I knew that for a long time he treated me in ways that I did not want to be treated, but I never realized that it was apparent to other people. I thought that I had always done a good job keeping up the masquerade... Perhaps it was just that Brian was so sensitive that he could perceive what others could not. Brian was shocked when I told him that I had actually thanked Andrew for being nice to me. He did not pry deeper into our relationship, but let me know that if there was anything that I ever wanted to talk about with him, that he was just a phone call away.

The second trip that week was with my friend, Roger. We were traveling to one of our suppliers and rode to the airport together. We stopped into Friday's for a drink before boarding the plane. He, too, had been at Laura's party. He confided that Laura's divorce surprised him, and he lamented that he thought they were good enough friends to have confided in him. He then turned to me and said, "You know, if there's ever anything that you want to talk about with me, I'm here for you." Wow, I thought. This was only 2 days after Brian said the same thing. Apparently, the masquerade was not as good as I had thought. It was either that or both of these men were more sensitive than I ever imagined possible. The only other man that I had ever known to be sensitive was my father. My hopes of having a man like him had been shattered years before. I regretted the mistakes that I had made but knew that I was unable to erase them.

On one particular evening this fall, I decided to sit with him and watch the movie he was watching. I sat quietly on the matching reclining chair that I had gotten him for Christmas. The movie was about a group of young adults who had been friends for a long time. Reunited because of the sudden death of one of their friends, they returned to the home that his sister had turned into a Bed and Breakfast. As the movie went on, it was apparent that one of Sid's friends was a boy who had dated Sid's sister in high school and part of college. He had returned for the funeral with his new girlfriend, who was eager to put to rest the fact that he had never gotten over Sid's sister. Cole was a Christian, who did not understand why Lucy had suddenly broken up with him during her third year of college. They had planned to get married when they graduated, but she suddenly broke up with him and said they could never be married.

As the movie wore on, there were many references among the friends, some of whom were Christians, and some of whom were not, to having a saving faith in Jesus Christ and allowing Him to forgive you for your sins. In the movie, Dwayne and the other Christian friends were trying to talk the others into attending church the Sunday after the funeral. One of the Christian friends was married to a very annoying Christian woman, who exhibited an obnoxious "holier than thou" attitude, often telling her husband that they should not be associating with the "sinners".

As the Sunday morning church service began, the pastor asked if anyone wanted to give praises or prayer requests. Lucy stood up with trepidation and confessed that the reason she had broken up with Cole when they were in college was that she had had an abortion, and she could not forgive herself. She ran with the wrong crowd and had a one-night stand that resulted in a pregnancy. She could see no other way out and sought an abortion, knowing that she would never be good enough for Cole.

The obnoxious woman was appalled and began to tell her husband that they needed to disassociate themselves with such sinners, to which he replied, "You just need to shut up. Do you not know that Jesus came to save the sinners? I love you, honey, but you cannot see that you are not any better than they are. And treating them that way isn't going to help them get to know Jesus"

The pastor was speechless as he tried to muster up words to say. Realizing that the best sermon had just occurred, he simply ended with an, "Amen. Let us pray". In the parking lot, as the group was saying their good-bye's, preparing to return to wherever life had taken them, the obnoxious lady asked them all to forgive her for being so wrong. The Jewish friend who had only come to be polite hugged her and told her that he forgave her, and that by seeing Christians can make mistakes after all, that he might think about attending a messianic church again. Cole's girlfriend left quietly, knowing that Lucy and Cole would eventually end up getting together. Cole hugged Lucy and told her that he forgave her. She handed him some roses from the rose garden that she had just picked. I sat there quietly, thinking about Lucy. I knew she would do it all different if she had the chance, but all she had were these roses to give, and they cannot help her make amends.

As I sat quietly watching the movie, a single tear fell from my eye, and in the darkness of the room, Andrew whispered, "I love you, Charissa. And I always have."

CHAPTER 18

Memory Lane

We packed the kids into the vans like sardines. A group of youth sponsors was taking a bunch of our youth group kids to the Winterfest Jam near Boston. I loved this part of town – it was where I had spent almost 5 years of my life while earning my degree. I was excited about the concert, not just for the music, but also for the kids who were coming. There were four different Christian bands playing – some play hard rock music, some playing hip-hop. Boston was the last stop on their winter tour.

During the ride down, the kids could hardly contain themselves as they talked about what songs they thought the bands would play. Allison was joining us for the first time. I was excited about that. We picked her up just before we were to meet the others at the church.

"Mrs. Jones, can you answer a question about Allison?" one of the girls asked, just before Allison got into the car.

"That depends on what it is," I replied. I was excited that Allison was coming with us, hoping that she would meet some girls her age from our youth group and feel comfortable enough to come back.

"Well, I heard that Allison carves things into her skin with a knife. That's what all the kids at our school say about her."

"Honey, I really don't think it is a good idea for us to talk about Allison that way. It is not our business to judge her. I want Allison to feel accepted by all of you. Do you think you could all do your best to make her feel welcome tonight?"

"Yeah, I was just wondering. So many people are afraid of her, but I'm not"

"She's a very nice girl. She may be hurting and looking for someone to care about her – let's see if we can show her Jesus tonight, okay?"

"Okay," Kristin replied.

Allison sat in the front seat with me for the ride down. We had the music playing very loudly in the car, and the kids were very excited about the concert.

As we turned down the road toward the parking garage, I pointed out the engineering building where I had spent much of my college career. It had been 17 years since I had graduated, but the building looked the same.

"Hey, Boston Psych is around here, isn't it?" Allison asked. "My dad made me go there once. Oh, yeah, look. There it is," she said, pointing out the window to the left. Boston Psych was almost directly across the street from the engineering building where I spent so much time. I never entered the building, but knew people went there for psychiatric evaluations. "Well, at least your dad cares enough about you to take you there, I thought to myself".

"See that building there?" I asked, pointing to my old school. "That's where I spent most of my college days." I looked at the entrance to the rear of the building. It was right near the canteen area where I had spent so many days studying. The vending machines provided the snacks and caffeine I needed to stay awake to study.

Suddenly, I found myself reminiscing about Steve. It was in that canteen that he said hello to me for the first time. My knees were wobbling like jelly beneath me. I was not even sure if I said hello back to him when my friend, Diane, said, "Hey! He said hi to you – that means he noticed you."

"Yeah, now all I've got to do is to get him to be my lab partner,"

I replied. I was joking, of course. I knew he would never be my lab partner – and anyway, I had already promised my friend, Dave, that I would be his lab partner. Diane had already taken the lab. Dave had asked me last semester to be his partner since he and I both still had to take the lab. The next semester would be starting in just a couple of weeks. It would be my last semester at UB before I would graduate.

I was not sure when Steve had started school at U of B. I surely would have noticed him before my junior year if he had been there. He must have transferred in from another school. I remember the day I first noticed him like it was yesterday. His gorgeous blue eyes and long eyelashes reminded me of Andrew's. He was taller and had darker hair. I had seen plenty of good-looking men but to that point, not one of them had ever made me weak in the knees. Where was he my whole life, I wondered to myself. I could tell that he was very intelligent, and though I was pursuing an engineering degree myself, his intelligence intimidated me. Steve was the kind of student who would challenge the professors when they were explaining certain circuits. I would see him studying in the library from time to time, but never worked up enough courage to talk to him. Although shy, I never intimidated easily. I was the one who asked Andrew out on our first date. Nevertheless, the thought of even talking to Steve made me weak in the knees. When I pointed Steve out to my friend, Diane, she said to me, "Don't you have a boyfriend?"

"I do," I said.

"Well, what are you going to do?" she asked.

"Well, probably nothing. There's no way that Steve would ever be interested in me," I said.

Several weeks later, on the first day of classes of my last semester, Diane and I walked into our EE1487 class. Spread out between the first two rows of seats were my friends Dave and Rick, Diane and myself, and Steve. After class, Dave asked me what day my lab class was scheduled. Since there were so many people taking it, they had scheduled one class on Mondays and Wednesdays and one on Tuesdays and Thursdays.

"I'm scheduled for the Monday-Wednesday class. How about you?" I said.

"Oh, I'm Tuesday – Thursday. That was the only class that fit my schedule. Rick has Tuesday – Thursday as well, so we decided we'd be partners if it's alright with you."

"Sure, it's ok. I'll find someone to be my partner," I replied. Diane had already taken the lab, so she did not need to take it this semester.

"Oh, I'll be your lab partner," I heard from my left. Diane and I were gathering up our books, ready to leave the classroom when we exchanged glances. Remembering the words that I had spoken just a few weeks prior, Diane nearly fell over when she realized that it was Steve offering to be my lab partner.

"Sure, that would be great," I said confidently. Inside, I could hardly contain myself. Because of the way everything fell into place, I knew that someone else had orchestrated the events. Steve and I exchanged contact information and arranged to meet before class the next Monday. Amazed at what just happened Diane and I walked out of the room.

Interestingly, I found that Steve was in exactly every single class I was that semester. We got to know each other quite well and spent much of our days together. I found out that he was six years older than I was. He had received a degree in Psychology and was pursuing his doctorate when he decided to become an engineer instead. He attended New Jersey Institute of Technology for two years before transferring to Boston to be near his girlfriend, who was studying Philosophy. Psychology is not even close to engineering. I wondered what would cause someone to make that dramatic of a change in his or her college plans.

As we began to know each other, he shared with me that he was agnostic, and I shared with him that I was a Christian. He challenged me to prove to him that God exists. I tried. I bought him

Masquerade

several books on the subject, and he bought me several books on Taoism and other world religions. We grew close over the semester. Every time I saw him, my heart would flutter excitedly. I never wanted that to show, though, so I put on a masquerade.

When his birthday came around in February, I asked him if I could take him to dinner to celebrate. He lived with his girlfriend off campus several miles from the school. It was a bit awkward when I picked him up for dinner and he introduced me to Cynthia. I wondered what she thought, but I really did not care. We ate at a wonderful little Italian restaurant, having a lovely conversation about many things. I was crazy about him, although I knew that his liberal and agnostic background and agnostic were not really a good match for me. That night, when we returned to his apartment building, he took me in his arms and gave me a wonderfully passionate kiss goodnight. I could hardly drive my car home. To this day, I remember that kiss as one of the best ever.

On graduation day, Steve asked me to sit with him for commencement. Andrew had to work that day, so he never attended the ceremony. My mom, sister, aunt, and uncle came. I wondered if Andrew and I would keep in touch after graduation. As the commencement ceremony ended and everyone began to throw his or her hats in the air, Steve grabbed a hold of me in an embrace that I wished would last forever.

"I have really enjoyed getting to know you. This semester has been my best ever. I hope you will keep in touch," he said to me. Are you kidding? I thought to myself. I never planned to let him get away.

Steve and I kept in touch over the next several years while he was in Boston. I went to work for that small company in East Hills, and he went on to get a Master's Degree in Electrical Engineering. We would meet periodically for dinner. He still lived with Cynthia. The last time that we talked was the night that I told him Andrew and I were engaged to be married. As he kissed me goodbye that night for the final time, he wished me a lifetime of happiness.

My happy retrospection came to an abrupt end as we turned left into the parking garage and the kids were loudly singing songs they anticipated hearing this evening. Allison Rae and the rest of the kids piled out of the car and excitedly climbed the hill to the event center.

The concert that night was awesome. Allison seemed to fit into the group really well and seemed to have a good time. To my knowledge, no one made her feel uncomfortable.

CHAPTER 19

Sunday Bloody Sunday

What took place on Sunday, December 5, was absolute proof positive that there is indeed spiritual warfare taking place all around us at all times, just as portrayed in Frank Peretti novels. As I had mentioned before, over the past four months, ever since the "bus" incident, Sundays have been a spiritual and emotional battle for me. Without exception, every Sunday for the past 15 weeks have met with tremendous oppression, suffocating my desire to play music and serve God. I have known with my head that it is a spiritual battle. However, I had been unsuccessful in conquering the feelings that so gripped my psyche.

The fight with Lisa that morning only hastened my typical "Sunday oppression" to begin in the morning hours rather than the evening hours of the day. Once again, she became possessive about which musicians were supposed to lead the worship service the following week. Pastor Ian had spoken to me the week before and let me know what songs he wanted sung. I had rehearsed them at worship band practice the night before. We were planning to lead music in the sanctuary service since Lisa's group would be leading in the youth service. When she asked about music for the next Sunday, and I told her that I had given the music to Greg and Ken, she exploded. She blurt out that they could not play because they "were not part of the original 'Adult Worship Team'". However, she mentioned that she "allowed" Martin and Logan (to participate because she wanted to. Martin and Logan were not part of the original team, either. In a fit of rage, she scowled at me and said, "The Adult Worship Team is MINE. I have been waiting a lot of years to see that come to fruition".

In my anger and frustration with Lisa that morning, in between the church services, I said to her, "you know, I think that you have misinterpreted what Pastor Charles meant when he said we are to be as 'ONE' worship team. I believe that he meant there was to be no strife between us, and you are creating strife. You know, I feel like I am just in your way!" With that, I walked away. Everything in me wanted to tell her that she could play for ALL of the services the next week – that SHE could figure out how to both accompany someone in the sanctuary service AND participate in the youth service as I unsuccessfully tried every week in November before concluding that it cannot be done. Honestly, though, I knew that would not be conducive to the situation, and despite outward appearances of the episode that transpired just before the third church service, I was not deliberately trying to upset any of the worship at the church. I knew in my head that Satan was trying his best to create a conflict. All outward appearances indicated to me that he was succeeding.

That afternoon, the oppression sunk me to depths that I had not previously seen. My mood and demeanor were utter despair, wondering why I had ever bothered with any of it. I canceled youth band practice for the evening, convinced that none of the youth would mind the break. This would have been the only practice in December. We had just struggled through the month of November, leading worship in the youth service. Week after week, the youth would show up late and unprepared for the songs. The music was terrible. I was frustrated with the kids and frustrated with myself for not making a bigger impact on them.

I had spent the afternoon crying softly and feeling sorry for myself. I knew that I looked as bad as I felt, so when it was time to take the kids to their Sunday evening church program, I just dropped them off at the front door and told them I would pick them up at the back door when it was over. As I drove over to pick them up, the oppression was overwhelming. I sat in the lower parking lot and despairingly decided that I would finally give up music. I looked at the dark pavement, shining from the light that shone on the puddle created by the all-day rain, and could distinctly hear a voice inside my head that I knew was not my own. As I was playing forward the conversation of my resignation, I could eerily hear the voice say, "oh, and I'm going to take my life". I knew with my head that the words were not my own, but the feeling was so powerful that I believe at that moment if there had been a gun available, I may have used it.

I slowly reached into my pocket for my cell phone, wondering what might happen next if there really was a gun in the car. I clicked the buttons to send a text message to Pastor Ian. "Satan is winning the battle. I think I am done with music. I'm sorry," I said.

"What's going on?" was the reply I received within a few seconds of hitting the "send" button.

"I do not know. It is the overwhelming Sunday depression," I said.

"Monday is my depression day," he replied, "and I'm praying for you real hard that Satan would have no authority and will leave you alone in the name of Jesus Christ."

"Thank you. And I will pray for you tomorrow." If I make it that long, I thought to myself. I thought to myself that it was somewhat nice to know that pastors are human, too, and fight the same kinds of spiritual battles that the rest of us fight.

Just then, the kids ran eagerly out of the church, excited to share with me what they had worked on while they were there. In addition, I mechanically responded with everything that I know in my head, saying nothing about the demons that lay inside me looking for opportunities to slay me.

CHAPTER 20

The Good Fight

The preparations for the celebration of Jesus' birthday have begun. Despite the spiritual battles that I could feel going on around me, I continued to prepare for Christmas as I had in previous years. Perhaps it was part of the masquerade; I needed to keep it up until I could once again feel solid ground beneath me. The depths of my spiritual battle with the demons of self-pity and despair had been fighting me for the past four months. I knew that the promise in the Bible, which I believed to be the complete and inerrant Word of God, told me that if I resisted the devil, he would flee from me but I was not sure how long it would take. I had been resisting for four months now. There were times that the battle was so long, and I so weary, that I did not think I would be able to continue to stand firm. In those times, I called out to the people that I have learned to count on – to Pastor Dwayne, and Pastor Ian, and Cooper, and John, and even the girls in my group, and asked them to pray for me when I could not. They interceded for me when I was too weak to fight myself, and I would return the favor for them when I was able to – I knew that.

I was up late tonight, preparing for a piano concert at Emerson United Methodist Church. They have invited me to come back to play for them every Christmas and Easter since I left their church.

The people were wonderfully thoughtful and had always been so good to me, but I feared that many of them had never truly asked Jesus into their hearts. As they were an aging population, I had often prayed and asked God to provide me with an opportunity through my music that I could reach them before they stood before the Lord. Instinctively, despite my depression, my work focused on sharing Jesus with them, wanting to help.

Because of my Sunday depression this year, I had found myself ill-prepared for the concert tomorrow. I knew that I wanted somehow to give an altar call. I had wanted to prepare a PowerPoint presentation to go along with the music, but since I have not yet picked all of the music that I would play, this would be impossible. I wondered if my Sunday depression would grip me tightly, rendering me useless in the spiritual battle for their lives. It had certainly crippled my ability to prepare. I had ordered small Christmas devotional books to give out with my CD's like I had done this past Easter; however, with no program to record, I did not have these ready, either. I guess I will save them until next year when I can prepare earlier. Hmmm, I thought. I am preparing in my mind for next year. Perhaps I am not ready to say Good-Bye after all.

The next day would be very busy, starting with three church services, and a visit to the local Assisted Living Center. Pastor Charles would be giving the message, and the group of musicians that I had been working with would be playing the songs we had rehearsed the Friday before, just as originally planned. Pastor Ian had helped to work that out a few days earlier, and we had rehearsed them tonight. I did not mention anything to the rest of the group about the fight that had occurred the weekend before between Lisa and me over the music.

Shortly before 2 AM, I went to bed. In the few short hours that I was asleep, I dreamed about a dark horse, thundering down from a forest that was behind my house. In the darkness, I could not make out the face of the rider, the horse, but the fury with which he rode foretold of the intense purpose for which he traveled. As the beautiful warrior trampled the twigs and leaves beneath his hooves, the world around was filled with an eerie silence which only exaggerated the deafening gait. The fog circled around the mountainside, as the sky behind the forest trees began to lighten. It must be almost dawn. In the stupor of sleepiness that comes with staying up too late, I lay in my bed praying that this dream meant that my depression had been defeated, giving way to the dawn of a new day. I hoped I had resisted the devil long enough and he was fleeing from me.

In his message that morning, Pastor Charles talked about the birth of the baby that was to save the world. He admitted that if he had been around when that happened, he would be tempted to dismiss the birth of a baby as nothing special at all. After all, millions of babies were born every year – what made Jesus so special? As he talked, I realized the similarities between his message and the words that I had prepared to share at Emerson Church tonight. I was convinced that only God could have orchestrated the coordinated theme.

That night, despite my ill-preparedness, I played with a confidence that could only have come from Heaven above. I allowed God to use my hands and heart to work for Him that evening, knowing that I was at the center of His will. As I prepared to play the arrangement of Silent Night with The Old Rugged Cross that lay on my heart, I was able to extend an invitation to those gathered in the church to make a commitment to Him this Christmas season. For the first time in four months, not a single thought of demons or self-pity entered my head. I had survived this attack from the Enemy, landing my feet on the solid rock of Jesus, my Savior. It had not been easy; many times, I thought that I would succumb to the pressure to give up, but I had survived by the grace of God.

The text message came in around 10 pm on December 13. It was from Aubrey. She said simply, "As of December 13, I have rededicated my life to Christ and turned everything over to Him".

AMEN. The angels in heaven were truly rejoicing. At this moment in Heaven, there was singing and celebration for the lost sheep that had come home. I had watched over the last several months as Aubrey was getting stronger in stronger in her faith. As the group in Let Go Let God has really gotten to know each other, and as sponsors and students alike have shared the areas of their lives where they struggle, I have felt God truly cement relationships. I have seen the students who have come through the program and entered the "aftercare" program really take other students under their wing. Aubrey has done this with Brianna; and it is so refreshing to see that, though we all face struggles, we all have people that we can count on.

I think back, for a moment, to the mess of a life that Aubrey was in just two short years ago. When I first met her, she was contemplating suicide; how I was concerned enough to talk with Pastor Ian about it. I remember asking him if he knew her at all. He said that he knew her very well, and was worried that one day she might try "too good" to commit suicide and accidentally succeed. That was when he first mentioned to me about his intention to bring Let Go Let God program to our church. As soon as he mentioned it, I knew I wanted to be a part of it.

This Thursday was the graduation for the fall session of LGLG. We have triumphed through many changes in the past few months, not only the kids, but the sponsors, too. We have reached out to each other and asked for prayer when we are facing battles. I have come to learn that every one of them when they are honest with themselves and each other, are fighting spiritual battles every day. The barrage of artillery comes faster and stronger the closer we get to the Lord and doing what He wants us to do, evidence that Satan is indeed worried that he will lose the war. Indeed, he will. I know this, with my head and my heart; but there were times that I could actually feel the demonic powers at work, preying on all of us as we were making an impact for the Kingdom.

I know that the battles are far from over; but I know that Jesus will prevail, and as long as we can be strong to weather the storm, He will carry us through, just as his word says.

EPILOGUE

Day-mare

Shock. That was my reaction.

"I did not see *that* coming."

I could remember Claire saying that regularly when she was 4 years old. She had been so precocious and made us all laugh. She had been the most outgoing child I had ever met. She lived her life to make friends. I remembered her first day of preschool. She had started a little bit later than everyone else because I had wanted her to be potty trained, even though it was not a requirement for the three-year-old program. I was a little worried that she would have missed the opportunity to meet the other kids in the class at the same time that preschool was new to all of them, too. We arrived at the classroom a little earlier than we needed to so that she could meet the teacher and find her seat before the other kids showed up. My fears subsided as she looked me in the eye and said, "Mom. You can go back to work now. My new friends are on their way here right now."

Moreover, she lived her life that way, looking for new friends to meet all the time. My friend, Kathy, used to tease me about the future, when Claire was inevitably going to look at me and say, "honest mom, I did not take the car out last night" but secretly deep down knowing that she was just hiding the truth. The Masquerade.

"I'm sorry to have to tell you this, Mrs. Jones." The next words that came out of the police officer's mouth seemed like they could not possibly be the truth. It all seemed so surreal. I almost fell over. I had to ask him to repeat himself, but not until I could sit down. It was as if sitting would make me hear and understand better.

The news sent shock waves up my spine. My stomach dropped and I felt like I was going to puke.

Just then, my daughter came running from the family room where she had been watching the television. "Mom! There has been a shooting in Penn Alta! The place looks like Dad's work! There are 7 people dead!" The words that the police officer had spoken replayed in my head, "There's been a shooting. Your husband is dead".

Officer Thompson relayed the details of the on-going investigation. I learned that at 2:17 PM that afternoon, a disgruntled customer opened fire in the shop of McGough's Car Service, the place where Andrew had worked for the past 17 years. Before turning the gun on himself, the gunman shot six other people, ranting angrily that they had "ripped him off". Among the dead were Joe Whalen, the service manager, Keith MacIntyre, a mechanic, and four tire-changes whom I had never met, and, of course, Andrew. The police asked me to come with them to the coroner's office to identify my husbands' body.

Nothing you can ever say or do can prepare you for a moment like this. The irony is almost laughable. I had prayed so many times, when our marriage was in shambles, that God would take him away from me. I have heard that it is common for people in bad marriages to wish and pray that their spouse would die. I had prayed this prayer for so many times before I became friends with Rob. However, God never granted it. Deep down, I knew that He had a plan, but in the midst of our crumbling marriage, I could not see it. When I finally was able to set aside my pain and surrender my marriage at Jesus' feet, then, and only then, was God able to begin working in my heart to prepare me to love my husband as he had intended. I remember with vague clarity the day that I finally knelt down beside my bed and asked God to either "fix it or release me from it".

I recall the moment when my prayers changed from, "dear Lord, please take him away from me and give me a man like so-and-so" to "dear Lord, fill my heart with the love for my husband that you intended me to have". It was as if a weight lifted from my shoulders. Accepting God's will for our marriage was an important step, not only for our marriage but also for my husbands' salvation. Many times, I had thought about the sin that we had in our life, and I wondered if that was what was holding Andrew back from accepting Christ as his own personal savior.

Deep down, I love him with every fiber of my being. When we attended the Rock Solid Marriage conference a few years ago, the speakers challenged us to take ourselves back to the time when we were dating, and to see if, way down deep in our hearts, we could get back to the feeling of love that we felt for each other back then. I was easily able to do that. However, in the daily grind and the busy-ness of the way our lives had become, it was hard to remember that feeling.

The healing of our marriage was not instantaneous – it was a matter of about 3-4 years. Through the healing process, however, I was able to see that God's grace was indeed sufficient for all of my needs. Over time, He gave me the grace to face my grumpy husband, and instead of criticizing him for being miserable, to love him for whom he was. Little by little, I began to have some compassion for him, realizing that each bad thing that ever happened to him during his life helped to shape him into what he was. True, he could have refused to be a victim of life's circumstance. He chose to allow it to fester in his life, creating cancer in him that slowly ate away at his soul.

My biggest fear had been that our children would unknowingly adopt his habits, and see the world through the jaundiced eyes that negatively colored all of his thoughts. I spent many hours on my knees praying that my children would follow my example and decisions and not allow circumstances to victimize behavior.

Wow. Over the past decade, our country had seen a rise in shootings. Events that were so uncommon when I was a child had become almost commonplace. The term "going postal", coined in the late 80's after several shooting incidents involving disgruntled postal workers, seemingly paved the way for lunatic behavior from sick people who had felt like society had wronged them. Victim mentality. The victims wanted other victims because "hurting people hurt people". Ever since the Columbine shootings in 1999, school administrators all over the country had participated in anti-bullying training and programs in the futile attempt to prevent such tragedies from occurring. What they failed to realize, however, is that unless and until they put God back into the public school systems, all of their attempts would be fruitless. Over the past several years, it administrators recognized that the socioeconomic makeup of the Northridge school district was almost identical to that of Columbine High School, and the school officials were acutely aware of the potential danger. They had mandated training for the teachers and administrators on how to handle these situations. They had begun anti-bullying programs and had anti-bullying slogans posted all throughout the school. I had always been somewhat prepared for the day in which we would experience a tragedy of that sort in our own schools. I prayed with my children every day before school, asking God to keep watch over them until they returned safely home. I prayed that if ever a shooting event took place, that my children would stand strong in Christ.

Even in my workplace, we taught a workplace violence class, and taught people to keep a watchful eye on the behaviors of co-workers for fear that one of them might someday be disgruntled to the point of making or carrying out threats. On several occasions, when we had associates that were terminated for well-documented reasons, the company has hired armed guards to stand at the door to protect the innocent workers in the event of a workplace violence issue. There had been a few occasions where disgruntled employees had, on their termination, uttered threatening remarks, either to burn the building down or to hurt the one who was terminating them. On the few occasions where I had the unfortunate responsibility to terminate associates, I recall the uneasiness walking from the building to my car, even in broad daylight.

Wow. Dead. How could that really be? When he left for work this morning, he was his usual, cranky morning self, irritated about the evening activities that would occur later that day. Why did it matter to him? It was not as if he made an extra effort to help chauffeur the kids to where they needed to be. He was just irritable that I would. Whatever, I thought, as he picked up his lunch box and closed the door behind. We did not even kiss goodbye. Of all the things that I wish I could do over again, at this moment, I wanted to go back in time 8 hours to the moments before he walked out the door. I would have handled it differently. I would have thrown my arms around his neck in an effort to be the one bright spot he had in his day. I would have told him how much I loved him and how happy I was that we had decided to stay married and work through our heartaches together. I would have.... I should have.... I failed to...

The Funeral

God gives us the strength to do what we have to do. Once I recovered from the initial shock of the news, police report, and body identification, I immediately went into task-mode. I did not have time to allow feelings to get in the way with the strength that I needed to show to my family. We had preparations to make; phone calls to friends, funeral arrangements, etc. Instinctively, I put a list together and delegated the phone calls. I asked my mom to make the phone calls to my side of the family. I made the calls to Andrew's side of the family. I called the funeral director and arranged to meet with him and Pastors Charles, Ian, and Dwayne. They had all been such an influence in our lives that I could hardly face this tragedy without all of them. I left the kids with my mom and headed for the meeting.

So surreal was the experience that it seemed as if I was really just watching all of the mechanical activities take place from somewhere above my body, looking down on all of the details as they were planned. There would be a viewing at Nieman's Funeral home – just for one day because that was all the longer I thought the kids could withstand. The pastors who were closest to us would take part in the service, and a salvation message and altar call given for anyone who wanted to surrender their life to Christ. Andrew's cemetery plot is next to my father at St. Peters Cemetery – the plot belonged to my mother, who has not needed it yet. He would wear the suit that we bought him last year. Funny, I thought. When we bought the suit, two new dress shirts, shoes, the suspenders and a fancy silk hanky that matched each of the shirts, the total cost came to around $700.00. Andrew looked at me and apologized for spending this much money all at one time. I told him I was thankful that we actually had the money to pay for the suit and did not have to put it on credit. I kidded him that one day we would bury him in the suit. Little did I know that it would be less than a year later.

As I wandered through the country roads that were so familiar to me, headed back to the place that had only truly become a home within the past few years, my thoughts turned toward my children. Claire, the baby, was now eight, the same age that I was when my own father passed away. What IS it with that age? That is when Brianna lost Trenton, Lindsay lost Morgan, and now Claire lost Andrew. It is an age of awakening.

Nicole would be sixteen in 2 months. Soon she would learn to drive... and go to her prom. She did not have a steady boyfriend yet, but she had a whole set of girlfriends who had been there for her since elementary school. They were truly like part of our family. I recall many of her girlfriends being afraid of Andrew when they were little. They said things to her like "aren't you afraid of your dad? He scares me." Nicole really was afraid of her dad. Her early years had left an impression on her young mind. She may not have known it consciously, but I could see it in her actions. She did not spend time with her dad unless she had to. She did her best to avoid conversations with him. I knew that he felt it because he had confided in me one time that it broke his heart. Without compassion, I had responded to him with a "what do you expect? You have done nothing with her since she was born! You never attended a T-ball game when she played T-ball. She swam on the swim team for 6 years before you ever attended a swim meet. She does not think you are interested in her life – why should she be interested in yours. You've done this to yourself!" Although I meant what I said, years later I realized that what he was trying to do by confiding in me was looking for ways that he could repair the broken relationship he had with his daughter. I succeeded in tearing him down, which did nothing for his own self-confidence, and left him feeling as though he should not bother trying.

Then there was David. He would be fifteen in January. He and Nicole were born just 11 months apart. I remembered with a smile finding out that I was already 3 months pregnant with him when Nicole was just 6 months old. What a shock that was! I remember taking all kinds of ribbing from the doctor, who said that we were supposed to wait 6 weeks after having Nicole before we tried that again! I remember the way in which Andrew found out, too. I would never live it down. I had taken several home pregnancy tests when things had not quite returned to normal after Nicole was born. Five of them, to be exact. They had all been negative. I called the doctor to ask if that was normal, and they said that indeed, it was not. They told me that I probably had a tumor or cervical cancer and that I should come to the hospital for blood work just to rule out pregnancy before they started other tests. Really? Wow, that was kind of a cold thing to say just like that over the phone. On July 3, I went to the hospital to have blood drawn for testing.

Fully expecting the results to be negative since five home pregnancy tests had previously been negative, I went home to wait for the results. When the phone rang, I expected the nurse to say, "your pregnancy test results are negative". However, what she said was, "you're pregnant". I was waiting for her to finish her sentence, and after about 5 seconds, I realized that she had. I had to sit down and ask her to repeat herself – it felt like a sitcom. I had barely hung up the phone and certainly had not recovered from the shock when the phone rang again. It was my sister, Stephanie. Sensing something was wrong in my voice, she said, "What's the matter?" "I'm pregnant," I said. She was elated and laughed like crazy. We talked for a few minutes and hung up the phone. Little did I realize that while I was still recovering from the shock, she was calling Andrew to congratulate him. I had not even had a chance to tell him myself. Crushed, he called me later, furious that he had found out from my sister. Though we moved on from that moment, I knew from the way that the subject continued to resurface even years later that it was something that hurt him deeply. I had not intended to hurt him – I intended to tell him first. I was all just in the circumstances and timing of it all – and it went so wrong. Epic fail.

David was born just 6 months later – 11 months after Nicole. The first few years of their existence are truly a blur... I developed a newfound respect for those who have twins. I had always wanted twins... now I had them, just 11 months apart. For all practical purposes, though, it was like having twins. They were both needy at the same time. As they grew, I did as many activities with them as I could. They were developing into wonderful young adults – minus some of the normal teenage stuff that we go through. I was extremely proud of all of them. Nicole and David had both consistently been on the academic honor roll, achieving the status of Highest Honors with Distinction every 9 weeks since 6th grade. They were swimmers on the swim team at school. Nicole was planning to start her first year as a lifeguard at the YMCA this summer – a job she dreamed about since she was about 10. Nicole played the clarinet – and had worked hard to become the first chair clarinet in the school band. Last year, she began taking guitar lessons, too.

David had developed into quite a musician also. He started playing the saxophone in 4th grade at school. By 6th grade, he was in the second chair and played his sax every chance he got. I remember the one year for Halloween; he dressed as a vagrant, and sat at the end of his friends' driveway with his saxophone case opened and a note that read, "Will play for candy". As people passed by, they reached into their bags of goodies and dropped candy bars and potato chip bags into his case. He was thrilled.

As I turned into our recently paved driveway, I remembered all of the winters that Andrew had plowed the driveway so we could get out. I remembered the winter that it snowed 23 inches in one night – and how a few days later when my van became stuck in a snowdrift and Andrew had to pull me out with a chain and his truck, I threatened to sell everything we had and move to Florida. He did not intend to move to Florida. So that spring, we began saving and working toward being able to pave the driveway. We finally had it paved last year. I laughed about those memories and briefly wondered who would plow now. Maybe David. Andrew still had the plow on his truck... The truck that cost $37,000 fifteen years ago – the truck that I said David would learn to drive on when we bought it all those years ago. Andrew had put a lot of work into keeping that truck – partly because new trucks are so expensive, and partly, I think, to honor the promise that he made to keep it around long enough for David to learn how to drive.

As I pulled up to the house and looked around at the recently mowed lawn, I couldn't help but think that there was no way that Andrew would have ever expected that would be the last time he mowed the grass. Almost numb, I pushed the large button on the garage door opener. As the heavy, white doors slowly climbed the track to reveal the 1970 Camaro inside the garage, I wondered if David would have the desire to finish the car that he and his dad had begun restoring four years ago. My mom had always said she would never live to see the day that it was finished. None of us ever dreamed that Andrew would not.

I entered the house to find the kids eager to hug me and talk about their dad. We spent the rest of that day reminiscing about the funny things that had happened in our lives, going through our photo albums to make a photo board for the viewing.

I had given my kids the same choice that my sister and I had with regard to our father's funeral. We chose not to attend our fathers' funeral. At the ages of 8 and 10, we thought that it would simply be too hard to do, and so we stayed at my grandparent's house with my grandmother during the funeral. All of my kids wanted to come to their father's funeral – the viewing and the ceremony. I respected their decision, knowing how difficult a day it would be, thankful that they would have the opportunity to say the "goodbye" that I never did.

They dressed for the funeral – David always loved to put on a suit – and he looked so handsome when he did. Nicole, whose main uniform is hoodies and flannel pajama pants, looked stunningly beautiful in the new black skirt and black and gray blouse that my mother had bought for her the day before. Claire, who had always been contrary regarding clothing, quietly dressed in the brown velvet dress that we had selected for Christmas this year. She never complained at all, even as she put on her cream-colored stockings and dress shoes. I hugged each of them tightly for what seemed like an eternity before we headed out the door for the funeral. I was thankful that the next session of Let Go Let God would be starting in a few weeks. Perhaps my kids would attend to help them deal with the grief from the loss they had just experienced.

The funeral home was packed. I had never seen so many people gathered in one place in all my life. I loved the way it smelled, with all of the fresh flower arrangements. I knew these hours on my feet would be exhausting, both mentally and physically. I was not sure that I was truly ready for it, but I knew in my head that God would give us the strength that I would need to get through.

The past few months have been incredibly difficult, spiritually speaking, but I emerged triumphantly from the battle. I know that through God's help, I was able to withstand Satan's powerful attack. I take comfort in the fact that future battles belong to the Lord as well. I am keenly aware that there will be future battles but am at peace knowing God will bring me triumphantly through them. My fervent prayer is that others will come to know the peace that passes understanding as well.

Made in the USA
San Bernardino, CA
28 April 2018